THE FELIXSTOWE MURDER

A 1940s Philip Bryce story

Peter Zander-Howell

To my super grandchildren -
Milly, Raffy, and Monty

FOREWORD

Philip Bryce is an unusual policeman. A Cambridge-educated barrister, he joined the Metropolitan Police in 1937 under Lord Trenchard's accelerated promotion scheme. After distinguished army service in WW2, by 1949 he has become Scotland Yard's youngest DCI.

Bryce has just married Veronica, a war widow whom he met during a recent case. His first fiancée was killed during a bombing raid in 1943, and for the last six years he had been envisaging a lifetime as a bachelor.

He is a very private individual, never talking of himself and wary of making close friendships. He is something of a polymath, with a remarkable fund of general knowledge – he has a habit of passing on snippets of that knowledge to people working with him.

INTRODUCTION

In August 1949, Detective Chief Inspector Bryce and his wife Veronica are in Felixstowe, on their honeymoon.

While they are taking afternoon tea in the Palm Court of their hotel, a man dies at a nearby table. Bryce quickly realises that he was poisoned.

Not wanting to get directly involved, nevertheless Bryce reluctantly agrees to a request from the inexperienced local police inspector to act as a sort of part-time consultant, thus turning the honeymoon ino a "busman's holiday'.

"Of all felonies murder is the most horrible; of all murders poisoning is the most detestable; and of all poisonings the lingering is the worst."
Lord Chief Justice Edward Coke
1552 – 1634

CHAPTER 1

Saturday, 13th August, 1949

Built by a local brewing family in 1902 and later bought by the Great Eastern Railway, the Metropole Hotel occupied one of the finest seafront locations in Felixstowe.

Once, it had been the accommodation of choice for the rich and titled of the day. Now, almost fifty years later, the Metropole was in decline. Requisitioned twice by the War Office, it had suffered when large numbers of soldiers were billeted in it during both wars. In between those conflicts, the Great Depression had all but ruined the hotel's financial footing.

Somehow, the Metropole had hung on. It still attracted guests to stay, particularly in its grand suites, and, despite post-war rationing, the hotel had also retained its reputation for elegant dining. This was partly achieved by nurturing excellent connections with local traders, most of whom were the descendants of the original grocers, butchers and fishmongers, who had supplied the hotel since its opening day. Fine food taken in dismal surroundings, however, is no great pleasure, and the ambience of the Metropole's exceptional Palm Court undoubtedly also drew custom to the hotel. The owners – lately the London and North Eastern Railway, and since nationalisation the Hotels Executive – had made a special effort to maintain this beautiful room, and its attractions were almost undiminished.

On this sunny August day, the hotel again welcomed partakers of the afternoon's refreshments, taking their ease amongst the exotic greenery of the Palm Court, and basking in the refracted light of its magnificent ceiling dome. An astonishing structure, the dome had been created from hundreds of pieces of clear, bevelled glass, all held together in an intricately patterned lead lattice. The effect in the room was quite wonderful.

Beneath this marvel of art and architecture stood two dozen tables of varying sizes, each draped with layers of palest cream, green, and lilac damask. Over these tables, quiet conversation and gentle laughter could be heard, as patrons relaxed and selected their sandwiches and scones, accepted refills of tea, and chose confections from the trolley.

This delightful ritual was startlingly interrupted when a scream was heard across the room. Neither those taking their tea at the hotel, nor the soft-footed waiting staff, were accustomed to interruptions – much less one so urgent and earsplitting. All around the Palm Court heads jerked towards the commotion. Everything stopped. The initial reaction of almost all the clientele was one of strong disapproval. Perplexed waiting staff frowned at one another.

In a corner of the room, a round table for six was flanked by two pairs of French doors overlooking the gardens. This particularly pleasant spot was the source of the scream: a young woman in her mid-twenties, with a look of utter horror on her face. Four of her companions each wore slightly different expressions, but all could be summarised as bemused astonishment.

The face of the last member of the tea party was quite different, but for the moment only the screaming girl seemed to have noticed this. The man to whom it belonged now fell from his chair and lay on the marble floor.

Sometimes, in the immediate aftermath of a sudden and shocking incident, a hiatus occurs. It is the period when those present must first grasp what has happened, and then realise that something must be done. Seconds ticked past before various people began to stand up.

Two girls at the table tried to calm and comfort their friend. Two young men knelt to tend to the man on the floor. One look at the casualty was enough to make them flinch. Although both had experienced the death of friends during the war, in the comfort of the Metropole's Palm Court it was totally unexpected, and somehow worse than either of them had previously experienced.

The taller of the men wore RAF uniform, with two and a half rings on his sleeve and pilot's wings above a row of medal ribbons. Standing up again, he called out loudly,

"Is there a doctor in here?"

His appeal for help had apparently been anticipated; a newcomer was already beside him. Ordering the man still crouched on the floor to move out of the way, the authoritative stranger took his place.

Moments later, he too rose to his feet. Beckoning two waitresses who had been serving nearby, he spoke quietly to the older of the pair,

"Telephone to the police at once; tell them it's urgent as there has been a death in suspicious circumstances". He handed the waitress his card, and tapped it with emphasis. "Make sure you tell them who I am."

With a final frightened glance at the body, she hurried off, relieved to be told to leave the room.

To the second waitress, who was studiously not looking at the body, he again spoke quietly,

"Find the manager and tell him not to admit any more guests. Tell him also to take the name and address of any non-resident who might want to leave."

This waitress was many years younger than her colleague (still at school, in fact) and waiting table part-time at the Metropole was her first job. She was a bright and capable girl, studying diligently for her Higher Certificate. Although aiming for a career above waitressing, she nevertheless worked hard during her shifts, and took pride in responding alertly to guests' needs. Now, however, she seemed stuck on the spot and made no attempt to carry out the instruction. Instead, she gave a mechanical reply:

"We do that anyway, sir. Take everyone's name and address when they book for afternoon tea."

The stranger, understanding the impact the incident had had on the youngster, lowered his head and fixed kindly grey eyes on hers before persisting:

"That's very good, my dear. But I expect the manager would like to know what's happening in his hotel. Off you go, please, and do exactly as I have asked. No-one is to be admitted; names and addresses are to be recorded of every non-resident – not just whoever made the booking."

Galvanised by his prompt, the second waitress now turned obediently and headed towards the door.

The five remaining members of the group had been close enough to hear these exchanges and were staring at him.

"Are you a doctor?" challenged the second man who, unlike his uniformed companion, wore a jacket and cravat.

"No. I'm Detective Chief Inspector Bryce, of

Scotland Yard. A doctor will have to certify death, of course, but I've seen enough dead bodies in the war – and since – to recognise one when I see it. And I've been in the police long enough to recognise the symptoms of poison."

These blunt statements of fact were met with stunned silence by the little group.

"The local police will take charge when they arrive," Bryce continued, "but in the meantime, please step right away from the table and touch nothing."

Seeing a fair-haired girl in the group reach for a handbag, he added sharply:

"No, ladies, that includes your bags; everything must stay exactly where it is. And for the moment, please do not leave the room."

The RAF officer, looking distinctly shaken and unhappy, nodded slowly:

"Yes, I understand." Pulling himself together, he proceeded to take charge of his companions, "Come along, all of you, there are some chairs over there against the wall – let's go and sit down." He ushered the three girls to the chairs, and the man in civilian clothes followed.

None of the other guests had heard the instruction to call the police, but the fact that a casualty was lying on the floor with the 'doctor' doing nothing to assist, could hardly mean anything other than that he was dead.

'Oh, poor chap! Only a young man, too,' they tut-tutted to one another sorrowfully. 'Still, these *things do unfortunately happen, you know. And life must go on, of course,'* they reasoned. Soon they were exchanging stories with their neighbours on adjacent tables about similar 'seizures' they had heard of.

Within a few minutes, most of the guests had resumed their previous positions and activities and, just as in one of Krylov's fables, managed to ignore the elephant in the room.

A most attractive young woman now rose from her table and approached the detective to quietly ask:

"Can I help at all, Philip? I assume this poor man's death is suspicious?"

"Quite right, my dear," her husband confirmed, "poison, I believe. You can certainly help. I want to talk to the people over there immediately, and although I have my pen as always, I have nothing to write on."

Veronica Bryce quickly looked around. An unoccupied table nearby was set for a large party of guests who had not yet arrived, and pristine menu cards lay waiting at each place. Gathering these up, she handed them to her husband with a smile and remarked:

"Enough space on the backs of these to begin with, I think?"

Accepting the cards, her husband returned her smile and made a further request:

"It's crucial that no-one is allowed to come near this table. If you can guard it until the local police arrive, that would be a huge help."

Although no one else seemed to have any desire to approach, Veronica Bryce decided to pace around the table, subconsciously acting like a bobby walking his beat. As she patrolled, her eyes moved alternately from noting the items on the table and their positions, to observing the nearby guests and waiting staff, as well as the group of five against the wall.

Leaving his wife in temporary charge of the ill-fated table – and by extension in charge of the dead man – Bryce pulled out a chair at the neighbouring spare table and made use of it himself. Retrieving his fountain pen from an inside jacket pocket, he quickly checked his watch and made a note of the time on the reverse of a menu card. Beneath this, he added his own observations and then tucked the card into a pocket.

These preliminaries completed, he joined the distraught party of five where they sat in a silent row. Positioning another chair to face them all, he sat down and proceeded to open the investigation.

"I'm very sorry indeed for your loss, of course, and I appreciate you are all very shocked at present; but I'm sure you understand that certain things must be done. It will save time all round if I can take some details now, before the local police arrive."

Nodding and murmuring indicated assent.

"Perhaps you would start, Squadron Leader. First, please tell me everything you can about the dead man."

"His name is Paul Farrow," replied the airman sadly. "Although he's in civvies today, he's a Flight Lieutenant at RAF Felixstowe, and a Sunderland pilot like me. He was twenty-six, an only child, and single. His parents are big landowners on the Norfolk coast somewhere near Brancaster, I think. I believe they're quite elderly and I can't imagine what a fearful blow to them this will be."

At this, the girl who had screamed earlier now started to shake with sobs. Her two friends led her a little distance away and once again tried to console her, whispering quietly.

"Thank you," said Bryce to the Squadron Leader, making notes as he spoke. "Now, if you would identify yourself, please?"

Taking stock of the officer before him, Bryce saw a clean-shaven man of medium height and build, in his late twenties or early thirties. A pair of large, strong hands, rested on his knees. Dark brown hair was neatly cut above a wide forehead and dark brown eyes looked straight back at Bryce as the RAF officer gave his details:

"My name is Brian Fisher. I'm a relative newcomer to the group, so I really don't know three of them. But I can tell you that the young lady who is most upset is Lydia Fitzgerald. She's a WRAF officer at the station. I know her quite well

9

from work, and Paul is – was – a member of my squadron." After a brief hesitation, Fisher decided to continue, "I don't think anyone will contradict me if I tell you that Lydia and Paul were very close; very close indeed. Not yet formally engaged, but it was expected that they soon would be." Fisher paused again, shook his head and lifted his shoulders to give a defeated little shrug, "Probably best if Jeremy takes over now and tells you about the others."

Bryce rapidly jotted down the relevant points the airman had given him, before turning enquiringly towards his companion who immediately offered:

"Jeremy Waller. And I'm literally the odd man out here, not being in the RAF. I used to be what Brian and Paul and even Lyd – Lydia that is – would call a 'pongo'. I'm a recently qualified solicitor." He inclined his head towards Lydia Fitzgerald, who was still being soothed and added, "The others are Deborah Jamieson – she's the blonde; and Emma Wade is the one with curly hair. I've known them for years." Waller stopped, as if unsure what more he could add, before supplying, "Emma and Deborah are both university students in London, back home for part of the holidays."

The solicitor sagged a little in his seat, "I really don't know what else I can tell you, Chief Inspector, except to say that I agree with what Brian said: that Paul and Lydia were very much 'together'. Emma and I are also very good friends, although from my point of view, unfortunately not as close as Lydia and Paul were."

"Thank you," said Bryce. "Incidentally, I was a 'pongo' myself, Mr Waller. Still am in fact. So I'm not likely to hold that against you!"

Bending over a menu card, Bryce wrote silently, giving himself a few moments to assess Jeremy Waller at the same time. He perceived a flamboyance about the solicitor that was completely absent in the Squadron Leader. The solicitor's sandy hair was styled with an abundance of hairdressing cream, rather than simply cut and lightly dressed. Unlike Fisher, who kept his nails trimmed and clean, Waller obviously preferred his own fully manicured and buffed. His choice of cravat and breast pocket handkerchief – collisions of geometric primary colours resembling a Kandinsky canvas – might have looked appropriately jaunty at the start of the tea party, but now they gave him a festive air which flatly contradicted the reality of events.

Bryce pressed on, "I'd like you both to think very carefully before you answer me: do you know of any reason at all why someone would want to kill Flight Lieutenant Farrow?"

Both men shook their heads, with Waller responding emphatically:

"No. Definitely not! And I'll go further and tell you that it's jolly distressing to hear you speak as though it's a foregone conclusion that someone wanted Paul dead. For that reason, I would ask you to justify yourself Chief Inspector – why are you so sure that this is a case of murder?"

The solicitor's tone had turned very quickly. His voice now had an edge to it; disbelieving and dismissive, with distinctly confrontational undertones. Bryce, who was practised in dealing with far more aggressive questioning from defence counsel in court, decided he would leave Jeremy Waller in no doubt about his thinking.

"Oh, it's quite clear to me that this is a poisoning," he stated confidently. "I can't see that ingestion by accident will need much serious consideration at all. And as soon as accident has been eliminated, the only feasible alternative to murder would be suicide. But..." Bryce shifted position and turned towards the rest of the room, "...look around you, Mr Waller. This would be a highly unusual setting to choose for a suicide, wouldn't you say? And that's before you take into account that the victim is a young man sitting beside his soon-to-be fiancée."

The Yard detective paused a moment to allow his words to make their impression on the solicitor, before developing his reasoning further:

"On top of which, I've never heard of a suicide in public which involved poison. That, and the fact that comparatively few suicides are carried out in public anyway, convinces me your friend was murdered – and in a particularly pre-meditated and cowardly way."

His explanation finished, Bryce

simultaneously raised his eyebrows and spread his hands, silently enquiring of the solicitor: 'what-more-than-that-do-you-need?'; then he sat back, waiting for a response. Jeremy Waller gave a begrudging nod.

The Squadron Leader had also listened closely to this exchange, and Bryce was sure that both men were coming to terms with his words. These were intelligent people, and soon – if they had not already done so – they would realise all five friends were suspects as well as being witnesses.

"The medical side will have to be confirmed by a doctor, of course, and there will be an autopsy," Bryce continued, "but I'd put a great deal of money on the result confirming poisoning – and I'm not a betting man."

Bringing his enquiries back on track, Bryce flipped over a new menu card and quickly drew first a circle, and then six squares around its perimeter. Turning to Brian Fisher he said:

"I need to know where everyone was sitting at the table. Perhaps you would describe the seating arrangements for me, Squadron Leader?"

Into each of the boxes Bryce wrote the names of the group members as Fisher recalled them. When finished, he passed the card back to the officer and asked him to sign it, confirming the seating was correct.

Next, he gave the solicitor a little job.

"I need to talk to the ladies. If you would ask them to join me?"

Jeremy Waller obliged with good grace. Following a few words with the girls, they returned to sit with the men.

"I'm very sorry about this", Bryce said again, looking closely at Lydia Fitzgerald. "The Squadron Leader and Mr Waller have given me your names and a little more information, but I still have to ask each of you this: can you think of any reason why someone would want to harm Mr Farrow?"

The three girls, all still very upset, shook their heads dumbly. Lydia had stopped crying, but she now looked quite ill and was leaning against Emma Wade for support. Emma herself, although dry-eyed, looked as if she'd taken a brutally forceful punch and might fold up at any moment. Deborah Jamieson appeared utterly wretched and had also been crying hard, judging by her smudged make-up and the dampness of the balled handkerchief she was churning around from hand to hand.

Bryce could see that further questioning of the three girls – particularly of Lydia Fitzgerald – was likely to be unproductive for the moment. In any case, each witness would soon need to be interviewed separately, and that wasn't his job.

He prepared to conclude his involvement by handing out five of the remaining clean menu cards and asking each of the group to clearly print his or her address, together with any other useful contact details. Fisher and Waller both produced pens, and the five silently carried out their clerical task in turn.

As they wrote, Bryce looked out over the rest of the room and observed a smartly dressed man moving smoothly from table to table. Hands clasped together, he wore an attentive and serious expression as he bobbed his head in agreement with whatever was said to him, before bowing and moving on to the next table. Bryce surmised this was the Metropole's manager, Mr Deacon, reassuring his patrons.

As Bryce watched the manager's professional tour of the room, two uniformed policemen entered the Palm Court. Standing briefly in the doorway to pinpoint the right table, they rapidly moved towards the corner French windows where Veronica was still slowly patrolling.

Asking the group of friends to stay where they were until the local police released them, Bryce collected their completed cards and moved across to join his wife.

"Good afternoon, sir", began the first policeman. A very well-nourished sergeant, he was completely dwarfed by his constable companion who was almost a foot taller but barely half his superior's weight.

"Now then, would you be Chief Inspector Bryce, sir?" he enquired in a broad Suffolk accent. On hearing the necessary confirmation, he continued, "I'm Sergeant Pryke, sir, and this here is Const'ble Edwards. I warn't fully sure what to do, so I took it 'pon myself to call in our CID chaps in Ipswich. Inspector Catchpole is coming directly. I hope I was in order?"

Bryce confirmed the Sergeant's action was the correct procedure.

"This is my wife, Veronica," he said, completing the introductions. "We're actually here on holiday for a few days. She has been guarding the body and the table while I've been talking to the witnesses over there."

The DCI indicated the sad little group which had reconfigured into two sub-sets since he had left them, all still seated against the wall. Jeremy Waller and Emma Wade were huddled closely together, whispering to one another, and were now a couple of chairs removed from Lydia Fitzgerald and Deborah Jamieson, who were seated on either side of the Squadron Leader,

"For now," Bryce continued, "I'll just put you in the picture, and then you are in charge until your inspector arrives."

He gave a concise outline of what had occurred and handed Pryke the completed cards, with details of the dead man and the five immediate witnesses all neatly recorded. Retrieving the card with his own observations from his pocket, and the seating plan, he passed these to the local officer as well.

"As an off-duty guest at the hotel, Sergeant, this is no longer a matter for me. It's up to you what you do until Inspector Catchpole arrives, but

I strongly recommend you get the police surgeon here as soon as possible."

Pryke vigorously nodded his understanding and motioned to Edwards, who was waiting ready with his notebook, that this was to be taken down.

Bryce continued, "And, if I'm right and this is a case of poisoning, then preservation of all the crockery and anything else on or near the table is crucial. I've told the ladies that they can't even have their handbags at this stage."

More nods and a crisp "Yes, I see, sir," from Pryke convinced Bryce that this would also be done. The Sergeant might have trouble outrunning a fleeing felon, but his eyes were sharp, and he was listening closely. Together with Constable Edward's rapid note taking, Bryce felt the two men were an efficient little team.

"By the way, I've also told the party of five that they can't leave until you, or your people, say so. I expect Inspector Catchpole will want to have them searched."

"You really won't be taking charge at all then, sir?" queried Pryke, surprised.

"Not if I can help it Sergeant, that's not my idea of a holiday," smiled Bryce. "Even if your boss decides to ask the Yard for help, it might not be me. But of course, I'll be happy to talk to your inspector if he wants. We'll be here for three more days – we don't leave until Wednesday morning."

Putting a hand under Veronica's elbow, Bryce said,

"I'll leave you to it, then, Sergeant."

With a farewell nod for the local men, the pair returned to their own table.

As before, Bryce sat where he was able to see what was going on in the rest of the room. Those on nearby tables looked curiously at the couple as they sat down again, but no-one spoke to them. Veronica's circling of the table and casualty had been noted, of course, and the arrival of the two police officers had naturally caused a fresh stir of concerned interest around the room. But guests agreed with one another that the manager had been *most* reassuring; and now that the 'doctor' and his pretty wife had also decided to carry on and enjoy the rest of their meal, they felt even more confident doing likewise.

"I guess the brew will be all but cold, my dear, but if you could just squeeze a little more out of the pot..."

Veronica had just completed this action when the waitress to whom he had given his card appeared and asked if they would like a fresh pot. Raising his eyebrows in question to Veronica, who responded with a shake of her head, Bryce declined the offer, and said they would be leaving in a few minutes.

"Thanks, Vee", he said. "I think it would be better if we are away from the room before the local Inspector arrives. The last thing I want is for him to feel under pressure unnecessarily."

As the couple used their lukewarm and

somewhat stewed tea to wash down another delicious scone apiece, it occurred to Bryce that he hadn't told his wife why he had booked this particular hotel out of those available.

"My parents often brought me to Felixstowe when I was a child," he reminisced. "We used to stay with relatives, all departed now. One day, when I was about twelve, we had afternoon tea here in the Palm Court. The hotel was closed to the public during the Great War and for some time afterwards, but was open again when we visited in the mid twenties. I've never forgotten this room – over three thousand square feet of beautiful marble floor, and this spectacular ceiling dome. It was the biggest and best room I had ever seen. Come to think of it, that's probably still true!"

"It's certainly an impressive room, Philip," acknowledged Veronica, "and I'm glad that the owners are able to maintain it rather better than they can in the rest of the hotel; but I guess it too must have seen rather better days?"

"Oh definitely," replied her husband. "Its heyday will have been the twelve or so years between opening and the Great War. Royalty came to stay in East Coast resorts like Felixstowe and Cromer back then. Even when I visited the Metropole over twenty years ago it must have already gone downhill a bit, although to me at the time it was just magnificent – so was the tea, as I remember.

"Unfortunately, its days as a hotel are

numbered; I guess it will close soon, and probably become the headquarters of some big company. I felt I just wanted to see it one more time; I hope that wasn't a bad idea. Going back to see long-remembered places can make one realise that nostalgia isn't all it's cracked up to be."

"Never mind, darling," smiled his wife, "I'm really pleased to be able to see some of the landmarks of your childhood. Though it's a pity this murder will give you an even stronger reason to remember the place." Her large green eyes shone as she grinned over the top of her teacup and added with faux seriousness, "I do hope our being here on honeymoon might also make it just a tiny bit memorable for you!"

Philip laughed affectionately and reached out to put a hand over hers, feeling a tremendous surge of pleasure as his fingers rested lightly over his wife's wedding ring finger. Immediately after his last big case in Hartminster, he had made the successful bid for the beautiful antique solitaire diamond engagement ring that Veronica wore. He was not an overly sentimental man by any means, but the twin symbolism of the durability of the gemstone, together with the continuity of the golden wedding band Veronica wore with it, held meaning for him.

"Shall we go, my love?" he asked.

They slipped away quietly without attracting the attention of the local policemen, dropped off their key at Reception, and went back around the building to descend the steep steps to sea level. Once on the Victorian promenade, they ambled along happily, hand-in-hand.

"When I came here as a boy", recalled Bryce, "the pier was half a mile long, the second longest in the country, I think, with an electric train running the full length. It was built by the same company that erected similar piers at Southwold and Lowestoft. They ran pleasure steamers between them, and to other places as well. Unusually, this pier was built of wood.

"But in the last war it was thought to be potentially helpful to the Germans for a landing, so the Royal Engineers blew bits of it up. I don't suppose it will ever be rebuilt now, alas. I'm not sure if the public are allowed onto it; but if we are, do you fancy a walk over the remaining two hundred yards or so?"

Veronica assessed the remains of the pier from where they stood, and shook her head. They continued onwards past the model yacht pond until they reached the end of the promenade. Pausing to consider the foreshore, Bryce remarked broodingly,

"I gather they've lifted the mines from the East coast beaches, but it'll probably take a long time before all the ugly concrete and iron obstructions are completely removed. Such sad reminders of the war. The sooner it's all cleared up, the better."

They turned to make their way back to the

Metropole. After a few steps, Veronica let go of her husband's hand and linked arms with him instead.

"Philip, I just want you to know that if you would like to get more involved with this case, that's absolutely fine with me," she said, pulling him a little closer as she spoke. "I realise that your work will make many demands on you and, just like today, those demands won't always be convenient. But I hope you know that I would never stand in your way."

"Bless you, Vee, that's very understanding of you," said her husband warmly. "But admit it now, you also want the chance to demonstrate your own detective skills again!" he said with a laugh, referring to the case which had brought them together just two short months before.

Without removing her arm, Veronica reached across with her other hand and gave his shoulder a playful swat.

"Anyway," Bryce went on more seriously, "the local force may not call in the Yard, and even if they do, I probably won't be given the job. I don't know Inspector Catchpole – our professional paths have never crossed – but as you heard me say to Sergeant Pryke, I'm happy to talk to him if he wants to pick my brains, such as they are. Or..." Bryce now stretched away from Veronica as far his arm would permit, "...I suppose I could just carry on with my holiday and lend you to him for a few days instead!"

Veronica spluttered with laughter before

coming to a standstill and turning her suddenly sober face upwards to look at her husband,

"A young man has just been murdered, darling, and although I know we are entitled to enjoy our special holiday together, I want the culprit found as much as you do, and as much as everyone who knew and loved him does. All joking apart, Philip, I'll contribute and be involved of course – if you genuinely believe I can."

Taking his wife's hands into his own, Bryce gave each of them a light kiss. No words were necessary, and they continued, arm in arm, to walk the full length of the promenade in the other direction, looking up at the tall Cliff Hotel as they passed. Just before reaching the end of the promenade, Bryce pointed to some buildings up a steep incline, well above sea level.

"You were only a child at the time, Vee, and perhaps didn't take too much notice of the ballyhoo, but that's where Mrs Simpson stayed for a few months, while she was waiting for her divorce court hearing in Ipswich in 1936. That divorce ultimately allowed her to marry King Edward – or rather the Duke of Windsor, as he had become by the time of their wedding."

CHAPTER 2

Returning to the Metropole via the roadway, they entered the reception area. From behind the desk, Roger Deacon saw them arrive. Without being told their suite number the manager produced their key and offered an apology:

"I'm sorry I didn't realise who you were before this afternoon, sir. I should like to thank you for the way you have kept things..." he paused to think of the right word "...restrained. Yes, restrained. An altogether terrible business and there's no point at all denying it. But it doesn't do to over-react, does it, sir?"

Bryce thanked the manager for the key, acknowledged the good sense of his remark and was turning to leave when Deacon quickly added:

"Inspector Catchpole asks if you would spare him a few minutes at your convenience. He's set up what he calls his 'incident room' in the Finborough Suite, just along that corridor, sir," he added, pointing.

"Very good, Mr Deacon," said Bryce. "I'll pop down and see him shortly."

The Bryces returned to their suite, where

poisoning immediately. What did you think?"

"Facial expression and lip colour, Doctor," replied Bryce. "I wondered about cyanide; but didn't smell anything. Mind you, I didn't get too close."

"I'm quite sure you're right about poison," agreed Quilter. "The apparent speed of death is certainly consistent with cyanide. And the fact that you didn't smell anything isn't necessarily significant, because a surprisingly high proportion of humans can't detect any smell from cyanide. However, I'll keep an open mind while doing the PM. As I've just been telling Catchpole, it's always possible that we will find more than one substance – or perhaps even something I've not met before."

Quilter turned to DI Catchpole,

"I'll let you know when I've finished, unless you want one of your men actually present?"

Catchpole declined this offer, and with a brief farewell to the detectives, the medic made his way out of the incident room.

Indicating the chair recently vacated by the police surgeon, the young detective inspector appealed to Bryce.

"If you can spare me a few minutes, sir, I'd be much obliged."

Bryce settled himself into the seat and appraised the DI in front of him. He was surprised to see the local man looked to be under thirty. Papers were organised tidily on the table before him, and with his neatly parted fair hair and crisp white shirt, Catchpole made a very good first impression.

Bryce himself had been promoted to detective inspector at the age of twenty-five, an unprecedentedly young age for the Metropolitan Police. But he had advantages no longer available to younger entrants even in the Met – the main one being that he had been recruited under Lord Trenchard's accelerated promotion scheme. Knowing that many county forces still relied to some extent on the Buggins' Turn principle of promotion, Bryce thought that Catchpole must have demonstrated an ability far above the average to have reached his current rank.

"I'll put my cards on the table, sir", began the young inspector. "It may be that someone more senior will be sent from County to take over here, or that the Chief Constable will decide to ask the Yard for help. But for the moment it's me. All on my own. And I don't mind admitting to you that I don't have any experience.

"I've only been a DI for a few months, and I've never had to tackle a murder case before. Never been involved with one, in fact. But I know enough to realise that everything I do – or fail to do – in the early stages, may help or hinder this investigation.

"I appreciate that you're on holiday, sir," the DI hurried on, "and you've already been incredibly helpful, preserving the scene and so on. But while you are here, if you could find a bit of time just to give me some guidance, or suggestions, I'm not too proud to accept, and I would be very grateful. Even half an hour a day," he added hopefully.

Bryce assessed Catchpole's words in silence for a moment.

"I respect you for saying all that, Inspector. There is a culture of guarding territory, so to speak, in many regional police forces. Professional pride can too often get in the way of asking for, or accepting, help. Personally, I'm in favour of a fully collaborative approach. So, yes; if what you want is a little input or oversight, then I am at your disposal – subject to a few conditions.

"First, you should know that my wife and I are on our honeymoon, and I don't think she would be happy if I abandoned her for any length of time. However, you should also know that in a previous murder case she helped me to such an extent that it's fair to say she provided the key ideas which led to the solution. So, I want Veronica included in inner circle discussions.

"Second, if you are superseded by a more senior detective, then of course I expect to be relieved of any commitment.

"Third, if the case hasn't been solved in three days, when we are due to leave, again I can't be expected to remain.

"Fourth, it must be made clear to everyone that you are in charge. If there is any kudos at the end it will be yours alone – I don't want to be mentioned." Bryce smiled, "The corollary, of course, is that you alone get the blame for any failure."

"All agreed," said the DI without hesitation, looking much happier. "Oh, and congratulations to you and your wife, sir," he added hastily.

"One thing does concern me a bit", admitted Bryce. "Am I right in thinking that your boss in Ipswich is aware that I'm here?"

"Yes, sir. The Superintendent who allocated me to the case mentioned your presence. I gather that when Sergeant Pryke rang, he told at least two people before he got hold of the Super. I imagine everyone in the station right up to the Chief Constable knows by now. And at Felixstowe police station too, of course. Does it matter, sir?"

"Well, only in so far as I have a suspicion the powers-that-be may think my presence means they don't need to find another more experienced officer to help you. If so, that would be very presumptuous, although I can't really blame them. Anyway, if that is the thinking it may or may not be to your own advantage!"

Catchpole gave a rueful smile. He understood the double-edged nature of his position perfectly. But he had made some quick enquiries and had learned that DCI Bryce was regarded as a very bright star at the Yard, and that one of his earliest successes had been the unravelling of the infamous Pimlico poisoning case; a case so unusual that once the dailies caught wind of it, Bryce's picture had appeared repeatedly in the press, both during the investigation and during the trial. Admittedly, the strange peculiarities of that case meant there was only one possible suspect from the outset, so that bringing the killer to justice had hinged entirely on the '*how*' and '*when*', rather than the '*who*' and '*why*'. Nevertheless, Catchpole was more than happy to place his faith in the Yard man's abilities in the current case, and he said so.

"Well, sir, I can only repeat that I'll be more than grateful for any guidance you care to give me. Perhaps I might outline what has been done so far?"

Bryce nodded, "Go ahead."

"As you heard, the Doc has looked at the body, and I've authorised its removal to the mortuary in Ipswich for the *post mortem*. We've taken photographs and so on. Detective Sergeant Jephson over there is getting on with the preliminary interviews. He'll get the basics down first: what each person saw; what was being said; what their relationships are; those sorts of things. When I've read the initial notes from Jephson's interviews I shall look for any discrepancies, and I'll talk to them all myself, but that probably won't be until tomorrow.

"Before he started, Jephson had each of the key witnesses escorted into this room one at a time. They were all searched over there," Catchpole indicated the corner with the screens. "Sergeant Pryke managed to contact an off-duty WPC in the town, and she came in to search the women. Thanks to you, none of them had been allowed to leave the hotel until they had been searched – nor did any of them use the cloakrooms before they were searched. Nothing untoward was found."

Catchpole checked some points on a page before him and carried on,

"Sergeant Pryke contacted the RAF Station Commander, so Farrow's next of kin can be informed; and so that the Medical Officer could make arrangements to look after Miss Fitzgerald who, assuming she isn't the guilty party, is naturally the most affected of the group. It turned out that Mr Fisher had already spoken to the M.O.

"Names and addresses for all residents and casual visitors to the Palm Court are automatically taken by the hotel at the time of booking, but the hotel only takes one name, that of the person who books. I told Pryke to go round and make a note of everyone's name before they left – because except for married couples we'd only know the name of one person in each party, and not the name of any companions."

Bryce made no interruption as Catchpole outlined events, but his initial favourable impression was being confirmed with each sentence from the DI. He was particularly impressed that the young detective had grasped the importance of recording the names of everyone taking tea. Clear thinking and careful method were both being deployed effectively by the detective.

"My next job is to go through all the items on the table in the Palm Court, which Constable Edwards is still guarding. None of the group – who I feel must be treated as the main suspects for the moment – had about them anything which could conceivably be used to transport poison, liquid or solid. So, I'm absolutely pinning my hopes that something on the table, or in one of the girls' handbags will give me some evidence to work with.

"If I may ask, sir, what have I missed that I ought to have done?"

Bryce, sat quietly for a few seconds, mentally reviewing what the inspector had told him. Presently, he looked at Catchpole and said:

"First of all, I think that everything you've done so far is correct. I also think you are right in your priorities."

Catchpole looked relieved, until Bryce added:

"However, on reflection I think I arrived prematurely at the conclusion that it was a fast-acting poison. In any poisoning case – and Quilter has no doubt that this is what we have here – it has to be remembered that the poison can be introduced by someone who is not in the immediate vicinity at the time the victim is either exposed to the poison, or succumbs to it. So apart from the people around the table there are two other broad possibilities.

"Much will depend on the speed of action of whatever poison we have here, of course. But, in case the first impressions are wrong, and it is instead comparatively slow acting, our first problem is that it may have nothing to do with any of the five other people around the table." Bryce allowed a moment for this point to sink in.

"The second consideration follows on from the first: I should have assumed from the outset that, for example, one of the waiting staff or even someone in the kitchen could be involved. That was my oversight."

Noticing DI Catchpole's raised eyebrows, Bryce expanded,

"I agree that may be very improbable in this case, where it doesn't seem likely that a waitress would have some poison ready to hand in case an enemy came in for tea.

"Even more improbable, I think, is that someone in the kitchen with a grudge could arrange so precisely – out of sight and at a distance – to target the victim. If this poison was quick-acting, as I believe it was, the greatest suspicion must still fall on those around the table. Nevertheless, along with the five friends, I should have segregated the staff who served at that table, and I apologise for that omission.

"It's too late to search the waiting staff now, of course, but I suggest you get someone to go through all the bins in and around the kitchen, just to ensure nobody has thrown out a container of any sort. Also, I suggest you add to your interview schedule any of the waiting staff who served, or even approached, that table. This is a small town, and it's always possible that one of the staff had some sort of relationship with one of the members of the group, including the deceased."

Catchpole immediately called across to his subordinate, Jephson, and gave swift instructions as advised, before turning back to Bryce:

"With respect, sir, I don't think you should blame yourself for the waitress thing," said Catchpole. "After all, if you hadn't been here, the five main witnesses wouldn't have been corralled, and the table wouldn't have been preserved. As it is, we know for sure that no one else approached the table, we have the cups, milk jugs, teapots, remnants of scones, cakes, sandwiches, sugar bowl, jams, etc. – absolutely everything – all untouched and ready to be analysed. And possibly some evidence in a handbag. But thank you very much for your thoughts anyway, sir. We'll see if anything incriminating turns up for Jephson."

"It would be really helpful if the *post mortem* could show clearly not just what the poison was, but how it was administered. Or, just as helpfully, identify how it couldn't have been administered," mused Bryce. "It will narrow things down properly for you."

Inspector Catchpole gave a slight groan and nodded. He would have preferred his first murder case to be rather more straightforward. Already he had five front-line suspects, and now the DCI from the Yard was hinting that there might be others in the hotel, and possibly many more outside. The DCI hadn't quite finished:

"Do you read detective novels?" he continued, "because a couple of Christie's fictional cases involving the excellent Monsieur Poirot come to mind. I don't say they have any relevance here, and indeed both cases really overstretch one's credulity. But my point is that a real-life detective mustn't assume that what seems to be obvious is actually true. Like M Poirot, we have to think unconventionally.

"In one story the situation was rather like today's – a group of people sitting around a table in a night club. The administration of the poison is unobserved.

"In the other story, a guest is poisoned at a party. There is no obvious motive."

"Oh Lord," said Catchpole. "Yes, I've read both of those and I quite see your point, of course. I'll try to query every apparent fact. I never thought detective work in a serious case would be quite as complex as a Christie story!"

"I've handled a few cases," said Bryce with modest understatement and a sympathetic smile, "and I can assure you that they aren't always complex. Sometimes criminals almost give themselves up, as the trails of clues and evidence they leave are so clear. Sometimes, a slice of luck or a happy coincidence will help you out. All I'm trying to do is warn you that there can be pitfalls."

Bryce didn't dampen Catchpole's spirits any further by pointing out that a slice of bad luck, or an *un*happy coincidence, were both also possibilities, together with other assorted impediments to success.

"I really appreciate all that, sir," said the Inspector.

"Very good," said Bryce, "I'll leave you to it then. Feel free to find me again anytime tomorrow, if you wish. By the way, I assume you won't be allowing use of the Palm Court again tonight, as you haven't cleared the crime scene?"

"That's right, sir, everything on the tea table is next on my list. But even with best efforts we won't be finished in time to allow dinner this evening, although we'll definitely be clear before the morning."

"I think Veronica and I will have to find some fish and chips on the seafront instead," said Bryce, not at all unhappy at the prospect.

"That sounds good, sir," said Catchpole. "I hope to have the same before the evening is out. Do you know the town?"

"Yes, I used to stay with relatives here, but this is my first visit since before the war," replied Bryce.

"Well, there's a chip shop on the road just behind the Pier Pavilion, sir – I can thoroughly recommend it. Or, if you want to walk a bit further, there's another just by the Felixstowe Beach railway station."

The DCI thanked the local detective for his recommendation and left him to his work.

***

Passing through Reception, Bryce again ignored the lift, preferring to take the stairs two at a time. Once back in their suite he found his wife as he had left her, still contentedly viewing the sea. She had dug his binoculars out of a suitcase and was using them to examine the horizon. Putting them down on a small table, she turned to greet him.

"Well, my dearest, what have you to report? Has the local sleuth upstaged you and solved the case already?"

Philip laughed as he kissed the top of his wife's head again and lowered himself into an armchair beside her.

"Hardly," he replied. "In fact, I've just made it more difficult for him!" He explained how he had been remiss about the waiting staff.

"Oh, come on Philip!" exclaimed Veronica loyally. "The County men are really lucky you were on the spot and did what you did."

"Yes, Catchpole was kind enough to say exactly that when I was beating myself up," said her husband. "Nevertheless, I'm not exactly inexperienced in these cases, and I should have thought a bit more. I suppose the reason is that, subconsciously, I wasn't really treating this as 'my' case – more like a bystander really, but that's no excuse."

"Did you establish a rapport with Mr Catchpole?" asked Veronica.

"Early days, but yes, I could get along with him. He seems a very competent man, but he's young for his rank and has no experience of a murder case – he was quite open about it – and almost embarrassingly keen to pick my brains. In fact, he'd welcome it if Suffolk called in the Yard, and he could work under me. I've said I shouldn't welcome being called in at all, but that I'm happy to advise, and so on, while we are here.

"In truth, Vee, I feel a bit sorry for him. I wouldn't put it past County HQ to assume that they've got themselves a senior Yard man on the spot without having to pay for him! And as that's hardly fair on poor Catchpole, I feel morally obliged to help him a bit. I gave him a couple of examples of Hercule Poirot's cases, to prime him about the distinct challenges of poisonings."

"Last time, we discussed the abilities of Conan Doyle; this time it's Christie," laughed Veronica. "Did you find anything to criticise in her books too?"

"Not at all," replied her husband. "Well, only to the extent that one has to suspend one's disbelief in some of her scenarios."

Philip explained the conditions under which he had agreed to assist. At first, Veronica refused to believe that her participation had not only been included but insisted upon. When she was eventually persuaded that her husband wasn't joking, she bounced out of her chair to fling her arms around him and gave him a hug.

"Now, we're going to forget about this unpleasant business for a bit. We're directly affected this evening, though, because we may have to find somewhere else to dine. How do you feel about fish and chips out of a newspaper?"

This suggestion found complete favour with Veronica, who commented that it would be nice not to have to bother with changing for their evening meal. Standing up, she held out a hand and drew her husband to the window, pointing out to sea and offering him the binoculars at the same time.

"What's that thing in the distance that looks like Marble Arch?" she asked.

"It's the Roughs Fort," he replied, "a defence installation from the last war. I've never seen it before, but I heard about it somewhere. I suppose from six miles away it does look a bit like Marble Arch, but it's actually made of two huge steel tubes, connected at the top and bottom and sunk onto a sandbank. I understand that the tubes are about eight yards in diameter and twenty yards long. There are several of these forts around the east coast. Most – like the Red Sands group – are around the Thames estuary, but this one was to help protect Harwich harbour, a vital port in wartime, of course.

"I believe at any one time there were upwards of a hundred men based on it – unlikely as that seems looking at it from here. Whereas the Thames forts were manned by the Army, for some reason this one was a Royal Navy responsibility. Actually, as naval personnel apparently have to be officially allocated to a ship, the fort's official name was HMS Fort Roughs."

Veronica looked a bit askance. "If I were in the Navy, I'm not sure whether I'd rather be on a ship which might get torpedoed, or on what sounds like ramshackle bits of metal bolted or welded together and probably sinking into a sandbank!"

Philip laughed. "Well, it's served well enough; it hasn't sunk into the sand in eight or so years. In fact, I believe it is still manned for some purpose or other. I don't know how many personnel lost their lives on these forts, but I bet the death rate was far lower than in warships, whether surface vessels or submarines – or merchantmen. Also, much less chance of being seasick, except for the trips out and back, I suppose. But I must admit I'm very glad I wasn't posted to one of the Army ones.

"Well, I'm feeling properly peckish now. Shall we venture forth to find some food? Catchpole has recommended a couple of likely places."

Once again descending to the promenade, they wandered along until they reached the pier with the Pavilion theatre in front of it. Leaving the promenade and re-joining the roadway, they almost immediately caught the unmistakable aroma of fish and chips, and soon found the source. This was the first occasion since the couple met that the prospect of a fish supper from a chip shop had arisen, and neither knew the other's tastes. However, each opted for cod and chips, with salt for both, and vinegar for Veronica.

Whilst waiting for their order to be pulled from the fryer, Veronica pointed to the blackboard and mentioned that she had never come across one of the other options chalked up: rock salmon. Her husband was able to tell her that it was a more palatable name for a small shark called a dogfish; and that some London chippies (which he frequented when working late) called it rock eel, instead. He admitted that as cod was always his choice, superior even to plaice, he thought, he had never tasted dogfish in either guise and so couldn't really offer an opinion.

The two carried their food, heaped first into greaseproof paper and then wrapped in several layers of the East Anglian Daily Times, back to the prom and settled themselves on a vacant bench near the yacht pond.

"Come on now, Philip," started Veronica. "If I'm to be involved in solving this case you'd better brief me on everything so far."

After blowing gently on a chip to cool it down, Bryce began to tell her what he knew. He gave the names and a brief sketch of each of the principal witnesses-cum-suspects, together with a precise summary of what he, Catchpole, and Quilter had said to each other.

This took some time, as Veronica interposed a number of questions and, of necessity, there were many pauses while he ate. At last, he stopped, gathered up all their papers, and walked to a nearby litter bin to deposit them. Returning to the bench, he sat down again. There was a silence for several minutes, Veronica mulling over the details he had given, and Philip content to sit and simply look at his lovely wife, counting himself fortunate that he had been assigned the Broughton Place case which brought them together.

Eventually, Veronica broke the silence.

"I know you've told Catchpole that he must check if one of the waiting staff had a prior involvement or motive; similarly, anyone working in the kitchen. I know that must all be done. But in my own mind, I'm eliminating them already. Based on the fact that you, and Dr Quilter, both believe it was a fast-acting poison, I'm taking the view that the assailant has to be amongst the five friends."

"That's an extremely definite position you're adopting, Vee, and very early on in the investigation, too," said her husband, not sure whether to be impressed or concerned by his wife's total faith in him and the police surgeon.

"Yes," Veronica agreed. "Extremely definite.

Chiefly because I think an experienced doctor and experienced policeman sharing the same conclusion means it is likely to be the correct one; but also because it has suddenly occurred to me that before tea I saw Mr Farrow with Miss Fitzgerald in Reception. There wasn't a thing in the world wrong with him then, Philip." Veronica turned to look at her husband, "That has to be significant, doesn't it? Surely, a slow-acting poison, just about to prove fatal, would already have been producing symptoms some time before Farrow even arrived at the hotel?"

Philip nodded. "That's certainly what I believe. But we really do need the toxicology reports all the same."

"Oh yes, I appreciate that," Veronica agreed. Another small silence fell between them before she spoke again and asked, "Are you planning to be present during interviews?"

"Absolutely not," replied Bryce. "Reverting to a Christie parallel; if anything, I hope to be like Poirot when he promised to solve the mystery of the missing banker, all without leaving his flat."

"I see," smiled Veronica. "That's the one where Poirot relied on Hastings to gather the information he required. Are you casting Catchpole in the Hastings role, or do you propose to despatch me to find the nourishment for your 'little grey cells'?"

"Oh, a combination of the two of you, I think," Bryce replied, as if giving serious thought to her playful question. "The trouble is, you see," he continued with a theatrical sigh, "I have a horrible feeling that my undoubtedly massive brainpower, together with Monsieur Poirot's methods, plus Catchpole's help, may still prove insufficient here. So whatever modest contribution you are able to make might indeed be welcome!"

This drew a merry laugh and a quick hug from Veronica, who then suggested they return to the hotel as the evening was turning chilly. Starting back, hand in hand, she presently observed,

"Of course, you don't look anything like the description Christie gives of Hercule Poirot. When I first saw you, knowing you were a detective, I thought of Ngaio Marsh's Roderick Alleyne. I have always imagined him as looking very much like you."

"Flattery gets you everywhere," smiled Bryce. He decided that he had teased his wife enough for the time being, and refrained from suggesting that if he were to be a Rory Alleyne figure, Veronica could perhaps model herself on some fictional female sleuth. However, she read his mind, and said:

"We've only been married for a few days, Philip, but if you dare to suggest I'm just as you imagined Jane Marple, I shall have to divorce you!"

CHAPTER 3

Sunday, 14th August, 1949

Over breakfast the next morning, Bryce was not particularly surprised to see Inspector Catchpole approaching their table in the Palm Court, which was again available for use. Introducing him to Veronica, Bryce invited the DI to join them in their meal. Catchpole sat down but declined to take more than coffee. An orbiting waitress quickly brought him a clean cup and a fresh pot.

"I'm really sorry to interrupt your meal, Mrs Bryce," he said. "However, I wanted to inform you of two major developments. This morning, a small tube of tablets was found in Lydia Fitzgerald's handbag."

The Bryces fixed their gazes intently upon the young detective. His news sounded exceptionally promising.

"The ladies' bags had all been tipped out and contents thoroughly inspected yesterday, soon after you left, sir. Nothing untoward was found, only the usual lady-like things. As a precaution, though, all three face powder compacts and lipsticks were immediately sent for analysis." He poured himself some coffee and continued,

"It was only this morning that a WPC picked up Lydia Fitzgerald's handbag again. As I said, the bags had all been eliminated and were waiting to be collected by the ladies. WPC Morgan told me afterwards that Miss Fitzgerald's was a style she admired and would like to buy for herself, so she had a good look at it, which included feeling the watered silk lining."

Catchpole shook his head slightly at this point and Veronica realised that he found it odd that a woman could be interested in a handbag's lining. Hidden inside and seldom seen, the attraction of a quality silk lining in a handbag was obviously beyond his masculine understanding.

"The tablets were in a small glass phial behind the lining at the bottom the bag," Catchpole went on. "When the bag was tipped out yesterday, the phial didn't appear, but WPC Morgan felt it lodged in one of the side creases of stiff leather at the base of the bag. I've had a look at the bag and a small piece of the lining isn't gripped by the metal frame of the bag, as it should be. The gap is wide enough to allow the bottle to be slipped in endwise, but then it would be stuck out of sight behind the lining and sort of wedged in place by the leather crease. That's why it didn't emerge when the bag was turned upside down yesterday." He paused to allow either of the Bryces to make comments, but none was forthcoming.

"That's the 'how' part of the crime, I believe. What I need to find out next is why Lydia Fitzgerald did it. The tablets have been sent off for testing, of course, and I've asked that they be prioritised," he finished."

Catchpole drank some coffee and managed a smile as he confided:

"I can tell you both that I'm suddenly feeling hopeful for a quick resolution to the case now, especially in view of what happened last night."

"You mean your other development?" queried Bryce.

"Exactly, sir. Last night, at about 7:30 pm, Flight Officer Fitzgerald complained of severe stomach pains. Fortunately, the medical officer at the base didn't like the look of her and arranged immediate stomach pumping. Knowing about the earlier incident, he also very sensibly retained the pump contents. Miss Fitzgerald was taken to the Felixstowe Cottage Hospital, but an hour or so later she was transferred to the Anglesey Road Hospital in Ipswich. She's still there, apparently out of danger now, but still barely conscious and very poorly."

"Oh, dear!" exclaimed Veronica with feeling. Bryce sat silently.

"The incident was reported to us by 9 pm last night," continued Catchpole, "but there was a communications failure. The matter wasn't linked to yesterday's murder until half past seven this morning. Unforgivable, really, as the M.O. called it in specifically because of yesterday's events, but there we are. Don't suppose we could have done much more overnight anyway; I didn't get to bed until midnight as it was.

"My Sergeant is searching Miss Fitzgerald's quarters as we speak," added the DI, "but the doctors won't allow me to talk to her until mid-afternoon at the very earliest. I'll tell you frankly, I'm hoping to get a confession, sir."

Catchpole drank more of his coffee and waited for some reaction from Bryce, who was looking very thoughtful.

"Any idea how long the tests on the tablets and so on will take?" asked Bryce.

"Pretty quick, I believe," said Catchpole. "We don't have all the facilities that the Met lab has, unfortunately. But if we sent the things to London, it would take days to get the results."

Bryce nodded, "Who does your testing?"

"We rely on chemists and doctors in the hospital for routine tests. I think they're competent – I'm told a couple of them have previously given evidence successfully in a murder case. Being local, they will also be quicker. But I'm worried that if we do have some unfamiliar poison, it could get missed."

"I shouldn't worry too much, Catchpole," Bryce told the DI. "Even if they test everything and still find nothing, it won't be too late to send material to the Met laboratory. But whatever was pumped out of Miss Fitzgerald should certainly be split, and a part retained for despatch to Hendon if necessary."

"Thank you for that suggestion, sir. I'll pass that on to the hospital."

"Just one other thing," added Bryce. "Do you know if Miss Fitzgerald was alone when she was taken ill? In other words, did she call the M.O. herself, or did someone else raise the alarm?"

"I'm not sure, sir. I'll have to check that."

"I completely understand your eagerness for a conviction," said Bryce, "but there are at least three possible explanations for Lydia Fitzgerald's current state, and one of them exonerates her completely – despite how incriminating the current evidence against her appears at the moment."

With his coffee cup replenished and once again travelling towards his lips, Catchpole now looked instantly deflated. Bringing the untasted cup back down to its saucer, he asked anxiously:

"What are your thoughts then, sir?" clearly concerned that his theory was about to be demolished.

Bryce leaned forward and flipped over his breakfast menu card. Uncapping his fountain pen, he again made use of the Palm Court's stationery and helpfully itemised his three possibilities for the Inspector.

"One: a genuine attempt at suicide by Miss Fitzgerald, now overcome by guilt, remorse, etc.

"Two: a deliberate ploy by Miss Fitzgerald,

hoping that her phial of tablets wouldn't be discovered, and to divert suspicion away from herself for the murder, becoming a victim, instead." Bryce looked up to see Catchpole was now smiling faintly.

"Yes, Inspector, both of those points support your contention that Lydia Fitzgerald is the guilty party, and I don't say that you are wrong about that. You must, however, keep an open mind whilst you wait for those test results. You can work out the third possibility by yourself, but I'll jot it down for you,

"Three: attempted murder of Lydia Fitzgerald by a person or persons unknown." Bryce slid the menu card across the table to Catchpole.

He pressed on. "Taking the first two possibilities together, whether it is a suicide attempt, or a red herring, designed to divert suspicion away from herself, there's a chance that the means of administering the poison will remain in her room."

"Agreed, sir," said Catchpole, "although I suppose if she is really cunning, she could have got rid of everything outside somewhere, just retaining a single dose to swallow later."

Bryce nodded approvingly.

Veronica, who had listened silently throughout, thought it was time she contributed to the conversation. Somewhat dissatisfied with the way the local detective had arrived at his conclusions about Lydia Fitzgerald's guilt, and not completely convinced by her husband's red herring hypothesis, she decided to play devil's advocate.

"But why would Lydia Fitzgerald try to divert attention in that way? She's a WRAF officer, so we can assume intelligent. If the tablets in her bag really are the poison as you believe, Inspector, she could never have realistically relied on the fact they wouldn't be discovered, could she? More significantly, why would she have even a small phial of tablets with her when you have just pointed out that she might be cunning enough to ditch any surplus tablets before taking a dose herself? Why take a bottle to the tea party at all, when just a single dose would have done the deed on poor Farrow?"

Catchpole nodded slowly, "Yes, I can see the logic in what you are saying."

Veronica hadn't finished.

"Equally worth considering is why Lydia Fitzgerald would jump the gun, so to speak, and poison herself before she knew for sure that the tablets *had* been discovered. From what you've told us, Inspector, without a curious WPC admiring her bag this morning, the tablets never *would* have been discovered, and Lydia could have collected the bag this morning, with absolutely no one any the wiser that a bottle of tablets was hidden in it."

Veronica shook her head, "No, I just can't accept that this was either a suicide attempt or a red herring.

"I'll go just one step further," she continued, "and I'll admit immediately that this is as much intuition, as it is based on my observations yesterday. When I was walking around the table I repeatedly looked over at the group and I can tell you I have never seen anyone more devasted than Lydia Fitzgerald. She looked destroyed by what had happened to her boyfriend. And just a short while before, I'd noticed them in the foyer when they arrived together. The way they looked at one another, touched and smiled," Veronica sighed and sagged slightly in her chair, seeing again the airman and his girlfriend in her mind's eye, "they were genuinely in love. I'm sure of it."

It was quite a speech. The three sat in silence for a few moments. Bryce was first to respond:

"But, if this is a double murder attempt, there remains the possibility that Miss Fitzgerald ingested the poison at the same time as Farrow, or at lunch, or even at breakfast. And for whatever reason – smaller quantity, or different metabolic rate, perhaps – it didn't act at the same speed."

There was a further glum silence as they all considered the ramifications of this scenario, and its most likely suspect, given that Farrow, Fisher, and Lydia Fitzgerald were all at the same RAF station, and would have taken many of their meals in the same mess.

"Well," Catchpole continued eventually, "I'll revise my earlier assumption and proceed on the basis that Miss Fitzgerald's poisoning is an attempted murder and keep my first theory in reserve. Given that, would you two, as my mentors, agree that at this stage I can safely ignore the possibility of there being two, separate, poisoners on the loose here? That we are looking for one individual who has struck twice?"

Both Bryces nodded.

"Right, I must get on. So far there's been no suggestion of finding a more experienced officer, nor of calling in the Yard. So perhaps I can come and find you again later this afternoon or this evening, sir? Hopefully we'll have the results of Farrow's PM by then, and perhaps I'll have spoken to Lydia Fitzgerald. I'd appreciate another little discussion with you both, if so."

"Given what happened here yesterday, I hesitate to invite you to afternoon tea", smiled Bryce, "but we'll be very happy to talk to you at your convenience. Even if we've gone out and about, we won't have gone far."

"Thank you, sir. And thank you, Mrs Bryce – not just for your own insights, but for allowing me to tap into your husband's experience." He stood and gave her a little bow before leaving the room.

When the Inspector was out of earshot, Bryce laughed,

"Another poor man entrapped by your wiles! But seriously, Vee, Catchpole will be glad of your help just as much as mine. Yes, I have the experience, but, as he just said, you have insight.

"Anyway, let's get ready and go out. It's

possible to take a ferry from the docks here, and go across to Harwich. Alternatively, and perhaps more interestingly, we could go to Shotley, on the peninsula between the two rivers. I've checked the timetables with the Concierge. It'll be very calm today – are you game?"

"Oh yes, lovely," replied Veronica.

Her husband considered the logistics.

"It's a bit far to walk after a full breakfast," he said. "We'll take the car to the docks, I think."

Bryce's only real extravagance was his car. Just after the war, he had bought an ex-Army staff car, a Humber Super Snipe, at a war surplus sale. However, its huge engine was very thirsty; and continuing – and varying – petrol rationing convinced him to change. Only a month earlier, he had bought a Triumph Roadster with the new 2000cc engine, in a beautiful burgundy finish. Although the engine capacity was half that of the big Humber and therefore represented a saving, it could still hardly be called 'economical'.

Both Bryces were silent during the short drive. Each of them, had they known it, was having almost parallel thoughts – alternating between *'how lucky I am to have found her/him'*, and *'how could poison have been administered to two different people, apparently in different locations?'*

They parked at the docks a few yards outside the railings of the RAF station. On getting out of the car, Veronica stood looking at a huge crane, seemingly standing on a stumpy pier jutting out from a broad concrete ramp, running between extensive hangars and the water's edge. Coming around the car to join his wife, Bryce said:

"You won't see many bigger than that. I remember coming down here to watch various seaplanes before the war, and my great-uncle telling me it's a 50-ton Titan. It's used, as you can guess, to lift seaplanes out of the water."

As he spoke, two Sunderland flying boats were swinging gently at their moorings, a few yards offshore.

"When it was erected, in the early thirties, I think, the seaplanes were smaller than those two – but I guess it could still lift a Sunderland as though it were a feather. They obviously planned long-term back then! I believe there is some sort of experimental station here, where all sorts of seaplanes are evaluated."

"So do those two aircraft have wheels as well as being able to float?" asked Veronica.

"There are such things as amphibious aircraft," replied her husband, but the Sunderland is purely a flying boat and has no wheels. When one of that type has to come out of the water the ground crew apparently provides a sort of temporary landing gear, and the crane lifts the aircraft out of the water and lowers it onto the wheels. I've never seen it done, though.

"Let's wander along to the dock and find the ferry," he suggested.

Philip led Veronica over various railway

lines to the edge of the small dock. Looking down, at the foot of some slippery-looking steps, they saw what appeared to be a raft floating in the water. Tied up to it was a small squat boat, bearing the name '*Brightlingsea*'.

"Is that our ferry?" she asked.

Her husband nodded.

"Improbable as it looks, like the hotel she is operated by the railway – once the LNER but now I suppose by British Railways."

Taking care over the lower steps which were partly covered in seaweed, they descended onto the floating landing stage and stepped onto the ferry. Philip gave their fares to the waiting deckhand. A handful of other passengers had already found odd places to sit. There was a tiny cabin, but it was a warm sunny day, and the Bryces tacitly decided to remain on deck, stand by the rail, and see the sights.

"What a good idea to have a floating dock," said Veronica. "Of course, I've seen the same sort of thing on the river in London – near Charing Cross, for example. I'd never consciously considered it before, but I can see now that this arrangement lets passengers embark and disembark regardless of the tide."

The Bryces, married only for a few days, already had the attuned minds of a couple who had been together for years. As Veronica stopped talking, and the ferry pulled out of the dock into the huge estuary, both instinctively transferred their thoughts to the previous day's murder – and what they both now suspected was probably an attempted murder. After a few minutes, Bryce said:

"Vee, I know you are thinking about the murder as well." His wife acknowledged this with a smile and a nod. "When you were guarding the table yesterday, can you remember seeing anything which seemed incongruous – you know, a rubber duck or a book on gardening, for example?"

Veronica considered the question with the seriousness it merited,

"I've been over this in my mind several times already," she replied. "As you probably noticed, I walked round and round the table, changing direction from time to time, so I got a slightly different viewpoint.

"But I saw nothing out of the ordinary. Absolutely nothing at all. There were the right numbers of cups, saucers, and plates. Each saucer had a teaspoon. Each plate had a knife. Two large teapots. Two milk jugs. Two hot-water jugs. One sugar bowl with a spoon. Two butter dishes, each with a butter knife. A bowl containing cream, also with its own spoon. A bowl containing some sort of jam, again with its own spoon. There was large platter half filled with sandwiches, and a two-tier cake stand loaded with scones. Two ash trays, both clean. Two of the plates – including Paul Farrow's – had half-eaten sandwiches on them, and the others had sandwich bread crusts and crumbs. They hadn't had time to start on the scones.

"Then there were the three handbags – one on the table beside where Lydia was sitting. The other two, rather more capacious, were under the other girls' chairs." She sighed, "But no dodgy-looking little bottle marked 'Drink Me' like in *Alice in Wonderland*, alas. It does seem as though the only potentially suspicious item might be the tube in Lydia's bag. I'm still hoping it's not, though."

Bryce thought that his wife, as he quickly told her, had a remarkably sharp eye, and an enviable memory.

"I would have to say the only thing that has struck me as the tiniest bit strange – and it really is only a tiny bit – happened before I came over and joined you," continued Veronica. "You remember how everyone stopped and turned to look when Lydia Fitzgerald screamed?" Her husband nodded. "Well, when everyone did start to move at the table, I thought it was a bit surprising that the girl sitting the other side of Paul Farrow, the blonde one, didn't try to help him. She walked straight past him and went to Lydia."

"Hmmm," Philip looked thoughtfully at his wife. "Some people are really not much use at all in serious situations; perhaps Deborah Jamieson is one of them. Or perhaps she just thought that Fisher and Waller would have more first aid experience, both having seen active service."

"Yes, that does make sense," his wife agreed.

"Are you glad it's not your case, darling?" she asked.

"Yes and no. I do find my – our – position rather unsatisfactory. If I were in charge, I'd automatically receive every piece of information, rather than being passed odd scraps. It's not that Catchpole is likely to hold back any evidence, it's just that he can hardly be expected to pass every snippet on to me. Also, I'd be able to direct enquiries to wherever I chose and talk to all the witnesses. No doubt Catchpole would be happy for me to do that, but then it would be no different to my taking charge, for which I don't have the authority – and more than half of me doesn't really want to do, anyway.

"Even when I was the junior detective on a case, I was always fully involved, not with the same responsibility as my boss, of course, but very much an integral part of the team. I do find the current arrangement rather trying, and I wonder if I made the right decision in agreeing that we would help Inspector Catchpole."

"You made the only possible decision," said Veronica. "Indeed, if the case isn't solved by the time we're due to leave, I seriously think we should offer to stay on a bit longer – assuming Catchpole still wants us. After all, you aren't due back at work for another ten days, and I don't have a job at all at present."

Bryce looked lovingly at his wife. "Thank you," he said, "I appreciate that. Let's see how things pan out."

By now they were halfway across the estuary, the confluence of the Rivers Orwell and Stour. It wasn't possible to see the geography clearly, because the water seemed full of warships moored together – lines with two and even three ships alongside each other. There were minesweepers, motor torpedo boats, corvettes, and a few destroyers, all left over from the war and now redundant. Despite the happy fact that the country was no longer at war, somehow it was a sad sight.

As the ferry dodged between the lines, the Bryces stood silently, watching. In no time at all, it seemed, the ferry arrived at Harwich and tied up at the landing stage there.

"We'll stay on board", said Bryce. "It'll leave on the next leg to Shotley in a few minutes."

Sure enough, another shouted order sent the deckhand scurrying to cast off the mooring ropes, and the engine roared again as the little boat moved off. After the ferry cleared the serried ranks of warships, the division of the waters became visible. To the left, one river disappeared into the distance, and to the right another. Between the two, Veronica could now see an apparently uninteresting bit of land. But quite close to the point and rising high above it was what appeared, incongruously as it was clearly on the land, to be a very tall and old-fashioned ship's mast. Bryce saw his wife staring at this oddity.

"That mast is in the middle of HMS Ganges, a shore establishment – what the navy people call a 'stone frigate' – it's to train youngsters joining the Royal Navy. I think they take them from about the age of 14 or 15. Climbing at least part of that mast is a compulsory element of their training. On ceremonial occasions it's covered in boys all the way up. Right at the very top, about 140 feet above ground, is a tiny 12-inch diameter platform called the 'button'. A very brave lad, known as the 'button boy', climbs all the way up onto that. There's a short post rising from the button, and when standing the boy can only hold on with his knees as he salutes. I watched that ceremony once, before the war, and marvelled then at the thought of what that climb entailed. I wouldn't reach the lowest yardarm, never mind the second or third – and certainly not the button!"

"Not for me either," said Veronica, with a shudder.

When the ferry tied up at the pier in Shotley, Bryce checked the timetable with the deckhand and found that unless they were prepared to wait three hours for the next trip, there wasn't time to disembark before the boat returned to Felixstowe.

They decided to stay on board. A few minutes later the little ferry left the pier once more and headed back into the estuary. Initially, the Harwich peninsula and moored shipping blocked the view towards Felixstowe, but in a while the huge hammerhead crane at RAF

Felixstowe came into sight in the distance.

Simultaneously, both switched off consideration of the water and the shipping, and once again began to think silently about the events of the day before.

CHAPTER 4

On returning to their car, they saw an envelope tucked underneath the driver's side windscreen wiper blade.

"Ooooh look, Philip – someone has left you a *billet doux*," laughed Veronica.

Her husband muttered in feigned annoyance. "And to think I gave such specific instructions that none of my legion of followers were to contact me whilst you were here with me!" he joked. "My guess is the same as yours Vee; this is from, or on behalf of, Inspector Catchpole. Pretty good police work, I must say, to find out the details of our car, and then to track it down."

Settled in their seats, Bryce tore open the envelope. Quickly scanning the short note inside, he shared the contents with his wife,

"It is indeed from Catchpole. He says that if we receive this before one o'clock, he'd appreciate it if we could call into the RAF station and find him." Bryce sighed. "As it isn't long after midday, I suppose we'd better oblige him. Looks like our lunch will be delayed."

He turned the Triumph neatly, drove back

the few hundred yards to the station entrance, and pulled up outside the guardroom. A corporal in RAF Regiment uniform approached the driver's side as Bryce wound down the window.

"Would you be Chief Inspector Bryce, sir?" he enquired. On receiving an affirmative answer, the corporal continued,

"I was told to look out for you, sir. You're to please make your way to the officers' mess over there." He pointed to a building not far away. "The local police are in there talking to the Station Commander. You can park right outside, sir."

"Thank you, Corporal," replied Bryce, and winding his window back, drove the short distance across the base to the building indicated.

"I'd better wait in the car, Philip," said Veronica.

"Nonsense," replied her husband. "The arrangement with Catchpole stands. In any case, a pretty lady is a welcome visitor in any mess."

Veronica appreciated the oblique compliment, and they walked arm-in-arm through the open doors into a hallway. Immediately, a white jacketed steward approached them.

"Good afternoon, Madam, Sir. May I assume you are the visitors the Station Commander and the Police Inspector are expecting?"

Bryce again agreed that they were, whereupon the steward invited them to follow him. They were led through a set of double doors into a large room, with a bar along one wall. A portrait of the King dominated the wall at one end, and Bryce noted that the remaining wall space was more or less covered with photographs of aircrew and aircraft – mostly seaplanes, with a few pictures apparently dating back to the Great War.

Scattered around the room, some by the bar, others in little groups seated at tables, were perhaps twenty men, almost all in RAF uniform. No women were present.

The Bryces saw Inspector Catchpole, sitting at a table near the front window. With him was an RAF officer with the four rings of a Group Captain on his sleeve, gallantry and service ribbons on his chest, and a 'handlebar' moustache on his upper lip. Beside him sat another man in civilian clothes. The steward stopped in front of the table and snapped smartly to attention.

"Sir, your visitors, sir," he announced.

All three men rose for Veronica, and Catchpole performed the introductions. It didn't surprise Bryce to learn that the apparent civilian was in fact the station Medical Officer. The Group Captain invited them to take a seat.

"Mrs Bryce, Chief Inspector, sandwiches have been ordered. Can I tempt you?"

Both Bryces nodded appreciatively. Without looking around towards the bar, the Station Commander raised his hand and gave a little wave. Within seconds, another steward, this one with a sergeant's stripes on his arm, appeared at the table.

"Dale, tell my new guests what you can rustle up in the way of sandwiches."

Sergeant Dale reeled off a list of possible fillings. The Bryces both opted for ham. On being pressed to select a drink, both chose a G&T.

"So," said the Group Captain, tweaking his moustache gently, "just a few words to set the scene. Welcome to RAF Felixstowe – although I could wish the circumstances were different. This is a terrible business.

"As you may know, this station has two partially overlapping functions – it's an ordinary RAF station equipped with Sunderland flying boats, and since the early 1930s it has also been an experimental seaplane station.

"Flight Lieutenant Farrow was an experienced and highly valued pilot. During the war one had to get used to losing aircrew. In peacetime, it's bad enough losing someone in an accident, but to lose one through foul play has been deeply shocking. And then we have the unexplained matter of Flight Officer Fitzgerald – we all pray that she pulls through.

"Inspector Catchpole here has explained your unusual position, Chief Inspector, and I sincerely hope that you and your wife will continue to work with him to solve this. However, I know I won't be able to add anything to your deliberations, and would only be in the way, so I'm going to leave you now with the M.O. I've issued a written order to all ranks, saying that you are to be given every assistance here. If you get any sort of obstruction from my people, just let me know. I appreciate that Squadron Leader Fisher is probably on your list of suspects at present, but he has my complete confidence and as you'll no doubt be talking to him, you might use him as a link with me – if that's appropriate and useful to you in any way. Oh, and I've instructed the senior steward that both you gentlemen are honorary members of this mess for the duration of the case. You are welcome to come in here at any time, and put any more refreshments you may have onto my tab."

Bryce and Catchpole gave their thanks and the Group Captain rose to go, turning to Bryce as he did so, he said,

"You're not a complete stranger to me, Chief Inspector. I've seen your picture in the papers from time to time, of course, but in fact I've seen you in real life before. You won't remember me, and I don't recall that we spoke, but we were both at some tedious military function in Berlin in 1945."

Bryce smiled. "I knew I'd seen your face, but I simply couldn't, for the moment, place you. I remember the scene quite clearly now you've jogged my memory for me! Just before my demob I got lumbered into working in Berlin. It was my fault – years before the war when I was applying for a reserve commission, I mentioned that I spoke some German. Much later, some beggar at the War Office looking for German speakers must have trawled through the old records."

As soon as the Station Commander had gone, Catchpole spoke:

"An update, sir. Farrow's death was caused by plain and simple cyanide poisoning. A massive dose; apparently of sodium cyanide. We'll get quantities and so on later, I hope. Analysis of the crockery, and remaining food and drink is not yet complete.

"Moving on to Miss Fitzgerald. She was definitely not poisoned with cyanide, although as the Doc here rightly suspected last night, she has certainly been poisoned with something. The hospital strongly suspects an alkaloid – probably aconitine – but there is apparently no test for that, so we may not be able to identify it for certain. She is now out of danger, and I'm going to visit her in hospital later this afternoon."

The Bryces absorbed this detail without comment, and Catchpole continued.

"This morning, sir, you asked whether she was alone when she became ill. The answer is 'no'. She was, of course, still in a very distressed state, and the Doc here had wanted her to stay overnight in the station sick bay. She argued against that, so as a compromise he agreed that she could sleep in her own room as long as she had someone with her through the night. One of her colleagues, Flying Officer Elizabeth Drury, took on that duty. They'd been together more-or-less constantly since Fitzgerald returned from the hotel. At about 6 pm, Drury went to the officers' mess to get something for both of them to eat, but Fitzgerald wouldn't eat anything, although she did have a cup of coffee and a slab of chocolate. She became very ill about an hour later, and Miss Drury rightly called for help."

Catchpole paused and asked, "Any comments so far, anyone?"

At this point two stewards arrived with the drinks and sandwiches. When all was arranged before them to the stewards' satisfaction and they had taken their leave, Bryce offered his thoughts:

"As we all know, cyanide is very fast-acting. The group had been sitting down in the Palm Court for at least ten minutes after their food and so on had been brought. So it is absolutely certain that Farrow ingested the stuff while he was actually sitting at the tea table.

"We are of course delighted that Lydia Fitzgerald has survived, but it has to be said that her case complicates matters no end. Aconitine, if it is that, doesn't work nearly so rapidly as cyanide. From memory, it could be up to an hour or so after ingestion before any sign appeared."

The Medical Officer, asked for confirmation of the point, spoke for the first time.

"Sorry to appear useless, but I'm no expert in toxicology. My only knowledge of poisons comes from a couple of lectures in medical school over ten years ago. Happily, until yesterday I've never met a case of poisoning other than run-of-the-mill food poisoning. However, I agree with what you say about timings, Chief Inspector. No way could poor Paul have ingested cyanide prior to entering the Metropole – it was taken, somehow, at the table. Equally, if it is aconitine, Lydia almost certainly didn't take her dose at the same table. Which, as you say, complicates things."

There was a further silence.

"Presumably you've interviewed Miss Drury, Catchpole?" asked Bryce. "Did she describe how the coffee was made?"

"Yes, sir," replied the Inspector. "Miss Drury says she went along the corridor to a little kitchen, taking a tin of dried coffee and two mugs with her. She boiled a kettle on a gas ring there, made the coffee, and returned to the room. Miss Fitzgerald already had some milk. We have of course seized the remaining coffee and milk for examination, but as Miss Drury also drank the coffee and took milk, they don't seem likely sources. Miss Drury had washed out the cups soon after they had finished drinking, so we can't prove the poison was in the cup at all. The wrapping on the chocolate was – as far as Miss Drury could see – intact until Miss Fitzgerald opened it. She also says that Miss Fitzgerald neither ate nor drank anything else while she was with her. I need hardly say that Miss Drury is very upset."

After another thoughtful silence, Veronica spoke.

"I don't want to sound alarmist, but here's a thought. There are two poisonings, apparently using different toxins, and inflicted – if that's the right word – at different times. I think we agree that the probability of having two independent poisoners at the same time is very low indeed. We have no clue as to motive, but both victims are closely connected. I appreciate that you must have the other four people around the tea table as suspects, but whether or not one of them is a murderer, what about a parallel possibility – that another one (or more) of them could also still be targeted?"

Bryce looked appreciatively at his wife.

"Good thinking, Vee," he said. "I guess you'll need to bear that in mind, Catchpole."

"Agreed," replied the Inspector. "It's crossed my mind that there is a scatter-gun approach to these attacks, almost as though the perpetrator doesn't worry too much about aim, and doesn't worry if anyone else is killed.

"But anyway, I need to advise the tea party survivors to be on their guard – although it would be ironic if in doing so we warn the murderer to avoid getting poisoned!

"Doc, I wonder if you could talk to your boss again, and get him to impose some sort of arrangement to keep an eye on Squadron Leader Fisher – perhaps something like you did for Miss Fitzgerald? I have a police guard on her at present, and whatever happens I'll get the hospital to keep her in for at least two more nights. I'll also contact the other two girls and Mr Waller. I want a further chat with them anyway."

The M.O. agreed to speak to the Group Captain. Bryce was still thinking.

"Do we know how Miss Drury was selected to watch over Lydia Fitzgerald?"

"I didn't order her to do the shift," replied the doctor. "As far as I know this is what happened. Brian Fisher very sensibly called from the hotel to pre-warn me. He brought Lydia to the sick bay on their return to the station. My staff called me. When I arrived a few minutes later, Brian was waiting with her. After I laid down my condition for releasing her, I went away to see another patient, and I didn't hear the conversation about who might be her companion. I assume Brian arranged that. But as Lydia outranks Liz Drury, it's even possible that she issued an order herself."

"Ah," said Bryce, "that's interesting. I haven't got the hang of these new female ranks. So a Flight Officer is higher than a Flying Officer?"

"I have to admit that I'm still confused," replied the M.O. It's only a few months since the WRAF came into being, replacing the old WAAF. But yes, a Flight Officer ranks with a male Flight Lieutenant, whereas a female Flying Officer ranks – believe it or not – with a male Flying Officer. Don't ask why some ranks are the same for males and females, and others aren't, because I have no idea of the answer.

"Incidentally, and I don't suppose this is relevant, but there aren't that many women on the station, and Lydia is currently the senior WRAF officer here."

"Hmm," said Bryce. "Look, Catchpole, you and I know that the majority of murders have one of three motives – money, love or vengeance. Some have more than one, of course. It seems to me that while you are waiting for some indication of how each poison was administered, perhaps some old-fashioned routine police work should be started. I know you are talking to the parties about relationships – and I respectfully suggest that should include discreet – or even direct – enquiries about former perhaps jilted boyfriends and girlfriends. Did Miss Drury, for example, have a fling with Farrow and hate him and his new young lady enough to kill them?

"That leaves money. So my next bit of advice is to get enquiries under way regarding the financial arrangements of each person at the tea table – and I guess Miss Drury should be included as well. In my experience, in normal times young men of Farrow's age rarely think about making a will. But service personnel, especially those who have seen active service, almost invariably make one. Squadron Leader Fisher told me Farrow's parents are prosperous people; if Farrow had any sort of means his will may be relevant."

"Yes, thank you sir. I'd probably have got around to thinking about that in a couple of days, but I'm glad you've raised the point."

Bryce hadn't quite finished. "If we forget

the matter of Farrow, and just think of Miss Fitzgerald's case in isolation, I wonder if there is another possible motive. It might be worth enquiring, via the Station Commander, probably, whether Miss Fitzgerald had made an adverse report on Miss Drury – or anyone else – recently. And perhaps whether Miss Drury might have thought that promotion could come her way if Miss Fitzgerald were to be eliminated?"

Inspector Catchpole sighed audibly.

"Oh Lord," he groaned. "Yes, you're absolutely right, of course. I may need to ask for a couple of extra plain-clothes men to help."

Veronica was wondering whether she should throw in another unpleasant suggestion. Eventually, she said:

"I gather neither of you policemen have ever come across two different poisons in the same case. That being so, and bearing in mind the scattergun approach you've pointed out, Inspector, surely there is a possibility that we could have a totally deranged mass poisoner?"

Not for the first time, a silence descended on the group.

"Well, Vee, again it's something more that Inspector Catchpole here will have to keep in mind," said Bryce. "All I'd say is that I know of no precedents in this country. There was Dr Palmer, of course, nicknamed the 'Prince of Poisoners', but although he was suspected of poisoning several people including three of his own children, he was actually only convicted of killing one man. In any case, he acted for financial gain, and certainly he was horribly sane as far as the law was concerned. Come to think of it, though, the crime he was charged with allegedly involved strychnine, but it was suggested that he'd used antimony to kill at least one of his children – so perhaps he is the nearest parallel to the two-poison killer we seem to have here."

Catchpole rose from the table.

"I need to get off to Ipswich to see Miss Fitzgerald," he said. "Thanks Doc – I hope I don't need to see you again, but I have a bad feeling that I shall. And thanks to you sir, and to you too, Mrs Bryce. If I get any more news, I'll try to find you either this evening or at breakfast tomorrow."

The others rose too, and after a round of handshaking, they all left the building. Catchpole's police driver had been watching for his boss to emerge, and brought his car to the entrance. The Inspector smiled self-consciously at Bryce.

"I still haven't got used to having a driver," he said. I sent him off with a couple of tasks while we were inside, but I'll have to work out how to employ him more usefully – or re-allocate him and drive myself."

"I sympathise," replied Bryce. "Like you, I usually work with a detective sergeant, and I tend to use him as my driver – although he is my passenger more often than not!"

"One last thing," said Catchpole. "It occurs to

me that it might be useful to know who arranged the meeting for tea at the Metropole, and how long ago that rendezvous was made. I'll make enquiries."

"Good thinking," said Bryce. "You don't need us, Inspector!"

The Bryces returned to their car. As they drove to exit the RAF station, a guard swung open the barrier and saluted smartly as they passed through. Veronica giggled,

"I know you're used to people saluting you, in the Army if not as a plain clothes officer, but I'm not. I could get to like it, though. Do you think they give commissions to married women?"

Her husband laughed as he steered the Triumph back towards their hotel.

"I'm absolutely certain that you'd make a very good officer, Vee. But all the services have inevitably been reducing numbers dramatically since the war – the sight of all those mothballed ships this morning is an illustration of that. Also – and don't take this the wrong way – I rather doubt if they'd take on a young woman of your age without experience. Not in peacetime anyway. If a new commission were to be granted to someone of your age, it would most probably be to an outstanding non-commissioned officer already in post."

"Oh, I know," said Veronica, "I'm not serious. I couldn't think of taking on a job which might send me to the other side of the world, so I wouldn't see you for months on end! And don't dare to say 'at least give it some thought'!"

Still chuckling, they reached the hotel and collected their key. When the Receptionist enquired whether they wished to take lunch in the hotel they agreed that the ham sandwiches had taken the edge off their appetites, and both decided against anything more to eat for the moment. On being told that the Palm Court would be serving afternoon tea as usual from 3 to 5 pm Veronica remarked,

"It's only 1:30 now, though, and I can't wait that long for a brew. Will you please send a pot of tea for two up to our suite as soon as possible?"

The Receptionist confirmed the request would be fulfilled within ten minutes, and the Bryces went up to their suite and settled again in the armchairs overlooking the sea. Philip spoke first,

"Well, my love, how do you feel about taking tea again in the murder room?"

"I think we should," replied Veronica. "There is just a possibility that we'll notice something this afternoon which triggers some sort of understanding as to what happened yesterday."

"That would be too much to hope for, but okay," replied her husband. "I wonder whether the Palm Court will be full of ghouls today. Even though news of the murder only merited a brief mention in The Times, it's splashed across the front page of the local paper, so everyone for miles around knows about it now. I doubt if people will be scared to take refreshments in there for fear of being at risk themselves. And, as P T Barnum allegedly said, 'there's no such thing as bad publicity'."

Each suite in the Metropole was equipped with a telephone. Picking up the instrument, he requested a table for two in the Palm Court for half past three.

Veronica had taken the binoculars from the table, and was scanning the horizon. Passing over the fort she had asked about before, she locked onto a small red vessel rather nearer the shore than the fort, lying almost straight out to sea from where they sat. She had noticed three similar ones at anchor in Harwich harbour that morning, almost lost in the rows of navy warships. Although she had never seen one before, she had immediately realised they were lightships. Now, looking at this one out to sea, with the aid of the powerful binoculars she read '*CORK*' on the side. It seemed an odd name for a boat, she thought, and mentioned it to her husband who was lying back in his chair staring blankly at the ceiling. He was the usual mine of information.

"It isn't the name of the vessel," he explained. "A lightship bears the name of the location it is sited in. That one marks the position of the Cork Ledge – another sandbank, I believe. But if it were to be moved, say down the coast to Kent, it would be re-labelled with the name of its new site – '*SOUTH GOODWIN*', for example. The name of the vessel, if it has one at all, is secondary.

"I was told about this lightship as a kid. Allegedly, you can see whether the tide is coming in or going out according to which way the lightship faces – and even without binoculars you can tell that from the shore by whether the mast, which is nearer one end of the ship than the other, is to the left or right of the lantern. But I don't recall which way round is which."

"Most interesting, darling," said Veronica. "You really do have a remarkable store of general knowledge."

"Maybe," replied Philip, "but I think we are going to need a lot of brainpower, not general knowledge, to solve our current problem."

A knock at the door heralded the arrival of their tea tray, and Veronica busied herself with the pot. Settled down again with their cups, she asked for some information on poisons.

"I've heard of cyanide, of course, but aconitine – if I've pronounced that correctly – is something I've never come across. But anyway, where on earth does one obtain deadly substances like that? Surely you can't just go into a chemist's shop and casually ask for an ounce of aconitine when buying your calamine lotion or rose hip syrup?"

Her husband's response was very serious.

"No, you certainly can't. For a start, an ounce of aconitine would be enough to kill dozens or perhaps hundreds of people. I don't remember exactly, but a fatal dose is about one fiftieth of a grain. Chemists are of course required to get people to sign a register when buying certain dangerous substances for which there may be limited valid uses – arsenic or strychnine, for example. The same is true of aconitine, which a chemist would probably stock for use in making up prescriptions – a doctor might prescribe tiny quantities for various medical reasons. But, other than for putting down a pet, I don't think there is any legitimate non-medical use, so I would hope any chemist would ask very searching questions before selling it over the counter.

"However, I think it might also be obtained from the roots of the monkshood or wolfsbane plants, quite common in England and abroad."

"Devilish," said Veronica. "What about cyanide – can that also be home-made?"

"I've no idea," replied Philip. "I do know it's found in the stones of fruits like cherries and apricots, and even to a lesser extent in apple and pear pips – but I don't know how you'd extract it. However, commercially produced cyanide salts are used quite legitimately, for example to destroy wasp nests, and also extensively in photography. I'm afraid that anyone could legitimately get hold of cyanide, and possibly a determined person with sufficient knowledge could adapt it as necessary.

"Cyanide in one form or another has been used to kill for centuries, and of course was used by the Nazis during the war. But aconitine has a history at least as long. In his '*Metamorphoses*', written around the time of Christ, Ovid refers to it as the poison likely to be used by wicked stepmothers on their stepchildren,"

"Charming!" said Veronica. "What about in real life, in more recent times?"

"Well, I don't know of anything recent, but there was a nasty case during the Indian Mutiny, where cooks added aconitine to the British officers' food. Someone became suspicious, and when the cooks refused to eat their own food, it was fed to a monkey. When the monkey immediately died, the cooks were hanged. It's also appeared as a poison in a short story by Oscar Wilde, and a character in Joyce's Ulysses uses aconitine to commit suicide.

"But actually, poison as a method of murder is remarkably rare, in this country anyway – although perhaps there are many more deaths which are never identified as murder.

"Anyway, if you'll forgive me, my love, this armchair is wonderfully deep and comfy, and I feel in need of a nap. Like Poirot, my grey cells require recharging!"

"Right," laughed Veronica. "You go ahead and snooze. I'm very content just to sit here and look at the sea, and perhaps read my book. I'll wake you in good time for afternoon tea."

In fact, Bryce awoke by himself an hour later. Feeling a bit rumpled, he excused himself and went to run a bath, thankful that when on holiday he was able to afford a suite with a private bathroom. It made a welcome change to the inevitable excursions along hotel landings and corridors to use shared facilities when he was away from home on police business.

In due course he re-emerged into the sitting room, feeling completely fresh. His wife looked up with a smile.

"So, how are the little grey cells now?" she enquired.

"Alas, they haven't produced any instant solution," he answered. "But it's almost 3:30, so let's go down and see if revisiting the crime scene helps."

They found the Palm Court quite busy, and the scene was much as it had been the day before. Most tables were occupied. Yesterday, in the far corner of the room there had been a round table to seat the party of six. In that position today were two separate square tables, each presently occupied by three ladies. Looking around the room, both Bryces noted that the ratio of female to male guests was something like five to one. Neither recognised any of the faces as having been present the day before.

Within a minute, the same waitress who had been semi-paralysed the previous afternoon arrived to take their order. She greeted them with a shy smile. After Veronica and Philip had given her their order and declined the suggestion of sultanas in their scones, the girl looked as though she was about to say something more, but then turned away towards the kitchens.

"I think she wants to speak to you, Philip," said Veronica.

"I'm sure you're right," he replied. "They're all very busy, so we really can't speak to her now. I hope she has something relevant to tell us, rather than just wanting to express sorrow at the incident, or to enquire about progress. We certainly need something. I don't know about you, Vee, but as I look around the room, I'm not yet experiencing anything like a '*Eureka*' moment."

A few minutes later the waitress returned with a trolley. She unloaded the various comestibles, together with the pots, jugs, and so on, required for tea. Having asked if everything was satisfactory, and been assured that it was, she hesitated again. Bryce nodded imperceptibly to his wife.

"Is there something you'd like to tell the Chief Inspector, my dear? Don't be afraid to speak," said Veronica, "because whatever you have to say may be very important."

The girl glanced around, and then blurted:

"I saw something yesterday which I only remembered later. I don't know what it might mean, but I thought I ought to tell the police. I've been wondering how to do it, and then you came in, sir."

"Quite right," said Bryce. "Why not just tell us your name for the moment, and then we'll arrange to talk to you somewhere quiet later on."

"Oh, thank you sir. I'm Frances Anderson. We're extra busy today, because lots of the guests who booked but couldn't come yesterday are here today instead. We're working flat out, and I shall be for the high jump if I stand here any longer."

"All right, Frances, don't worry. What time do you finish work?"

"Half past five today, sir."

"I'm guessing that there's probably a very good rule saying you can't go to a guest's room," said the DCI, "so what I suggest is this. We'll meet you in Reception just after five thirty. Then perhaps we can go and sit on the prom."

The waitress nodded quickly, smiled her thanks, and sped off to another table.

"What do you think, Vee?" asked Bryce.

"I think she's genuine. Whatever she saw, at the time it obviously didn't register as anything unusual. You know she wasn't herself when Farrow died, and it's hardly surprising she couldn't think clearly then. Later, she must have gone over events in her mind. Anyway, let's hope that whatever she tells us is significant and moves the enquiry forward."

"Indeed, but I'm not too happy about the ethics here. Effectively, I'm about to interview a potential witness. Not only do I not have the authority, but I specifically told the Inspector that I wouldn't get involved with interviews."

"Oh, come on Philip," responded Veronica.

"All we have here is a girl asking to speak to you. You could hardly refuse to hear her story. Anyway, she may have no useful evidence, in which case it would be a waste of time for the local police to bother with seeing her. Also, she chose you rather than contacting Catchpole or his sergeant – even though they are only down the corridor somewhere. I'm sure she will find it easier to talk to us than she would any of the others – she's nervous, after all. And finally, if you decide she needs to make a formal statement, then that's the time to inform Inspector Catchpole."

"You're right of course. As we sat here yesterday," he continued, "I noticed our group over in the corner by the French windows. They stood out, because apart from the waitresses they were by far the youngest people in the Palm Court. Even I was probably twenty years under the average age in the room, and you below that. And as you can see, that average has risen again today.

"But I can't say that I really took in much else – except that every time I glanced in that direction they always seemed to be enjoying each other's company. I saw no sign of an argument, or friction, or anything. The only face I couldn't see directly was the victim's, as he had his back to us. Although we weren't far away, the background noise stopped me from hearing any of their conversation, unfortunately.

"Anyway, I gave Sergeant Pryke my outline of the seating plan, but as I recall, Farrow was sitting between Deborah Jamieson and Lydia Fitzgerald who was on his left. Then, continuing around the table clockwise sat Mr Waller, Miss Wade, and finally the Squadron Leader. That doesn't get us very far, except that it must be easier for one of his immediate neighbours to poison him."

"Yes," agreed Veronica, "and as it seems that Miss Fitzgerald had poison in her room well after the hotel incident, I suppose that inevitably pushes her up the suspect list."

"But if she was intending suicide, we're left with the question: why choose a different – and less efficacious – medium?" queried her husband.

"We have to assume the police body searches were thorough, so even if she had any cyanide left over, in the hidden tube for example, she couldn't have taken it away with her could she; so she had to use something else?" Veronica speculated.

"I still can't buy the idea that she intended suicide, Vee. If she'd wanted to kill Farrow – and God knows why she should – and then herself, surely she would have dosed herself at the same time as administering it to Farrow?"

"Yes, I can't really argue against that," Veronica agreed. "Except to say that, if she is the culprit, her state of mind must have been badly unbalanced. Or, perhaps, for some reason she could only get hold of enough cyanide for a single dose." After a pause, she dismissed her own idea, "No, there's no logic in that – she could have taken the aconitine with her, of course."

"Hmm," said Bryce. "But anyone who knows enough about poisons to acquire or manufacture fatal doses of two varieties is likely to know about the timescale for their action. So there was little point in taking aconite at the tea table. Even if the dosage was fatal, it wouldn't have worked for some time. Anyway, I think Miss Fitzgerald's grief at her loss was absolutely genuine."

"Yes, I'm only being Devil's Advocate again," said Veronica. "I actually think you are right!"

Bryce smiled. "There's a lot to be said for hypothesising unlikely scenarios, and then working through them to see the flaws. Nevertheless, at present we certainly can't exonerate Miss Fitzgerald completely.

"Anyway, we have an hour or so before meeting Miss Anderson. If you're happy, we could take the car down to Felixstowe Ferry – that's in the opposite direction to the docks. It's only a ten-minute drive, probably less."

CHAPTER 5

Having agreed that a little drive would be pleasant, Veronica briefly returned to their suite to collect a silk head-square for her hair. The weather was wonderful, and another ride in the tourer, this time with the top folded down, appealed to them both.

Bryce handed his wife into the car, and took his seat at the wheel.

"One of the many things I love about you is your penchant for throwing out interesting tidbits about whatever we happen to be passing," said Veronica, "so I hope to hear more this afternoon – if there's anything of interest, of course."

Philip smiled to himself. Certainly, his general knowledge was extensive. However, his familiarity with their current location was largely because of his regular childhood visits to Felixstowe, and the kindly relations who had spent time showing him the sights he was now enjoying again with his bride. Had they been in, say, Scarborough, or any one of a hundred other places, he would have known next to nothing. For a moment, he thought about sharing this most relevant fact with Veronica, and disabusing her of her impression that he was some sort of oracle. But he decided against, confident that she would all too soon learn of his limitations. In the meantime, he wanted to enjoy her delight in him for as long as possible.

As they left Old Felixstowe, and passed through 'The Dip', the road dropped down to sea level.

"The man generally agreed to be the world's best ghost writer – or perhaps I should say writer of ghost stories – M R James, set one of his tales around here," Bryce announced. "Odd title – It's called 'Oh Whistle, And I'll Come To You, My Lad', written in the early 1900s, I think."

"Not my favourite genre," replied Veronica. "I know his name, of course, but I've never read any of his books."

"To be honest, neither have I," laughed her husband. "That's just a snippet from my mine of useless information. My uncle told me about it – and outlined the horror story – when I was here as a kid."

He waved vaguely at a tower on the seaward side of the road. "Martello tower," he said, without further comment, rightly assuming that Veronica would know something of the history of those.

Coming to a stop at what seemed to be the end of the road, they saw a somewhat ramshackle collection of huts and small boats. Either side of the road were two rather more solid public houses

– the Ferry Boat Inn to the left, and the Victoria to the right. Given the evidently tiny number of permanent residents in the vicinity, Veronica wondered aloud where their clientele came from.

"I really don't know," replied Bryce. "As you see, it's not an easy place to get to at the best of times, and during the war, this whole area was closed to the general public. I imagine the beaches hereabouts were only cleared of mines and obstructions recently. Over there," he pointed across the River Deben in front of them, "you can see the top of Bawdsey Manor. That was a top-secret research station, where they worked on radar. Actually, it probably still is hush-hush, so now you know about it, darling, I'm afraid I shall have to shoot you!" he said amiably.

"Anyway, assuming the ferry here was still open for people working there, maybe there were sufficient drinkers to maintain these pubs.

"One of the things I loved as a boy was watching a steam operated chain ferry, which could carry a horse and cart, and presumably later a car. The man who owned Bawdsey Manor in the 1890s installed it. His name was Quilter, same as the police surgeon here. Unusual name; perhaps they are related. I suppose the chain ferry became too expensive to maintain, but sometime in the 1930s it was removed, replaced by a simple motor launch. Pity in a way – I remember it puffing and clanking across the river. And the new boat couldn't carry a vehicle at all.

"Anyway, as I can't even see the ferry at present, and we don't really have any time for a walk along the shore, I guess we'd better get back for our meeting."

***

They returned to Felixstowe the same way they had come, and Bryce parked the car in front of the hotel.

"It's almost half past five now," he said. "Time to meet Frances, assuming she hasn't changed her mind."

As they entered the hotel foyer, the young waitress was just emerging from somewhere at the rear. She looked fretful and the Bryces correctly perceived that she had been having second thoughts about speaking to them.

"Hello, Frances," said Bryce warmly, determined to put her at her ease as quickly as possible. "Thank you for agreeing to talk to us. Let's find a bench on the prom and have our chat."

They walked down the steps and in the gardens below found an unoccupied shelter with U-shaped seating each side. The trio sat down, Veronica deftly manoeuvring Frances so she sat almost opposite them.

"Okay, Frances, I appreciate this is all a bit difficult for you, so we'll break the ice by talking a bit about something else first. I'm Philip Bryce, and as you know I'm a detective from Scotland Yard. This is my wife, Veronica. She helps me with some of my cases, so you can talk freely in front of her."

Veronica leaned forward with a friendly smile and offered her hand to the shy girl.

"Tell us a bit about yourself," suggested Bryce, "and remember, this is just an unofficial chat. So don't bother with 'sir' and 'madam', just treat us as family friends who have your best interests at heart."

"Thank you," replied Frances. "You're very kind. Well, I'm seventeen, and I go to the grammar school here. I take my Higher School Certificate next summer. My ambition is to become a lawyer, perhaps a solicitor, like Mr Waller – or maybe a barrister. I know Mr Waller's girlfriend slightly 'cos my big sister Amy was at school with her, and Emma's told me about some of the work Mr Waller does.

"I'm sure my husband won't mind my telling you this, but he has a law degree and was a barrister before becoming a policeman – still is a barrister, of course, although he doesn't practise now."

Bryce smiled. "Actually, there are far more barristers who don't practise than there are working ones. It's always been a useful stepping stone to other careers – a good number of Members of Parliament are barristers, for a start.

"If I could offer you a little advice, it would be this: as soon as possible you must buy or borrow a copy of a book called 'Learning the Law' by Granville Williams. In it, he covers pretty well everything you need to know. He's an academic barrister, rather than a practising one, but his points are applicable generally. The book has only been out for a couple of years, so hadn't been written when I was taking up law, but I like to keep abreast of all things legal, so I've read and enjoyed it." Bryce tore a page from his pocketbook, scribbled the title and author's name on it, and handed it to Frances.

"Sounds fascinating," said Veronica. "I'd like to read that book myself, Philip – perhaps I'll even try for the Bar one day."

"Well, I certainly have a copy somewhere. It was on a bookshelf in my flat. When we get sorted out in our new home, it's bound to emerge from one of the packing cases and you'll be able to read it.

"Anyway, Frances, we'd better get on and hear what it is that you'd like to tell us. I should say that although this is informal, I must of course pass anything important on to Inspector Catchpole. He may then need to talk to you, and you'd probably have to make a proper statement."

"Yes, I understand," replied Frances. "Well, I just want to tell you what I saw. Mr Farrow's lady friend was sitting to his left. I'd put down the teapots and so on. We have different sized teapots for one, two, or three people, so for a table of six we'd use two of the largest pots. Some guests expect the staff to pour; others don't. Anyway, they started to pour the tea themselves, and I moved away. But a minute or so later, as I was clearing another table nearby, I happened to glance up, and saw Mr Farrow pass a little glass thing – it looked like a sort of tube – to his girl friend. She took it and shook something out into her own tea. I didn't watch any more, and I didn't think about it again until this morning. I just registered it had happened without thinking it might be important. It's not that unusual, you see; recently a few guests have taken to using some sort of sugar substitute, sugar still being rationed, of course. And it probably still isn't suspicious, but I just thought I should tell someone what I saw. Now that I have told you though, it all sounds a bit silly and unimportant."

"Not at all, and thank you very much, Frances; you were right to tell us," said Bryce. "Let me think for a minute, and perhaps I'll have a question or two."

"Presumably you didn't see if Mr Farrow was given – or took – anything from the tube himself?" asked Veronica.

"No, I didn't, I'm sorry," replied the girl.

"You have nothing to be sorry for," said Bryce. "It's good that you have reported what you did see. But I also assume that you didn't see where the tube ended up – in other words whether it belonged to him or her or indeed to anyone else?"

"No, unfortunately I didn't," replied Frances.

"No matter," said Bryce. "What you have told us may be very, very important – we can't know yet."

There was a silence for a minute, Philip and Veronica each trying to assess what significance Frances' report might have. The young waitress looked from one to the other. Eventually, Philip smiled.

"Frances, we'd both like to thank you very much for coming forward. You were absolutely right to do so.

"Now, our car is at the hotel – would you like a lift home?"

"Thank you again, but I can probably walk home in the time it would take to reach your car and drive round," the girl replied.

With a reminder that she should contact either them or Inspector Catchpole immediately if anything else should come to mind, the Bryces said goodbye to Frances and set off for a little walk towards Cobbold's Point, and the would-be lawyer turned to go in the opposite direction.

***

Neither Philip nor Veronica spoke for the next few minutes. Turning back at the end of the promenade, they remained silent until they returned to the same shelter, and by tacit agreement sat down there again.

"You'll have to report this to Inspector Catchpole, of course," said Veronica. "Although there's still no confirmation that the cyanide was in that tube, if it was then it's a great pity that

Frances didn't actually see the victim take – or be given – the pills or whatever they are."

"Yes; I'll try to contact Catchpole as soon as we get back, although I expect he'll come to find us later anyway. But if the tube did somehow contain the poison, Frances saw Miss Fitzgerald actually shake some into her own tea, and that could be highly significant."

"And, as you implied to Frances," responded Veronica, "the ownership of the tube is crucial, assuming again that it was the source. We know that Inspector Catchpole found the tube in Lydia Fitzgerald's handbag. But Miss Fitzgerald must confirm the tube was hers – unless she herself is guilty, of course."

"Ah well, let's get back to the Metropole," said Bryce. "We can perhaps have a drink in the lounge and then dine in the hotel if that's okay with you? Fish and chip shops won't be open on a Sunday, of course."

"Fine by me," replied his wife. "Home it is, James!"

After clambering up the steep flight of steps to the hotel, they collected their key at the desk and Bryce asked the Receptionist whether any policemen were still in the Finborough Suite. Hearing that there were, Veronica opted to leave it to her husband to report what Frances had seen. She took the key from her husband, and told him she would wait upstairs.

CHAPTER 6

Bryce walked the few yards to the incident room, tapped on the door, and went in. He immediately had a feeling of *déjà vu*. The scene was almost identical to that on his previous visit. Inspector Catchpole was sitting talking with Dr Quilter, just as before. Sergeant Pryke was in another corner, engaged on the telephone, again exactly as before. The junior CID officer was still sitting at his same table, and the only difference was that he didn't have an interviewee tonight, but was simply writing.

Bryce saw that the Inspector was looking harassed. However, on seeing the Scotland Yard man his brow cleared and he smiled a welcome.

"Do come and sit down, sir," he called. "Since lunch I've acquired a lot of information, although there really isn't anything positive."

"I have a snippet for you too," said the DCI, "but let's hear your news first."

"Well, the Doc here has been making contact with the hospital chemists. Easiest if he tells you about that."

Quilter nodded.

"Even though Farrow's teacup was overturned, there are still traces of cyanide in it. There is no trace of cyanide in the unfinished sandwich on his plate, nor in anything else on the table he might have used. Therefore it's pretty certain that he was poisoned via the teacup. The time between swallowing cyanide and showing the symptoms would only be a matter of seconds, and death would occur within a minute or so at most.

"As you know, Catchpole here found a small glass tube of tablets in a handbag. They are sweeteners – a sugar substitute called Dulcin. Popular in Germany, I understand, and although I don't think they are on sale over here yet, I guess it wouldn't be difficult to get hold of them. With restrictions on sugar, I know a few people have looked for alternatives – sodium saccharin has been around for years, of course.

"However, I fear the tube may be irrelevant. There were seven tablets remaining in it, but no trace of cyanide in any of them – nor in the dust at the bottom of the tube.

"Turning now to Miss Fitzgerald's case. She still isn't fit to be interviewed, unfortunately. Apart from the poisoning, she has been given a sedative to mitigate severe shock. The hospital says the Inspector can go in tomorrow morning, when they think she'll be able to talk.

"It simply isn't possible to say definitively what toxin she took, but the hospital chemists are adamant that it is one of the alkaloids. Many of those are very nasty substances – morphine and cocaine, to name two. This was very probably aconitine. Unfortunately, unlike many toxic substances – arsenic, for example – there is no chemical test for it. I'm told that some years ago there was a doctor who swore he could differentiate between various alkaloids by taste alone, but I really can't see any court allowing an expert witness to testify on that basis!

"My assessment is that the girl is very, very lucky to be alive. Lucky that she had someone with her, too, and also that her M.O. was on the ball.

"In Miss Fitzgerald's room Catchpole's sergeant found a bottle of – you've guessed – Dulcin tablets. A rather larger bottle than the tube in her bag. But I'm afraid, there was no sign of either cyanide or aconitine in any of the remaining tablets. Cyanide is easy enough to identify, but quite reasonably no one in the lab felt like sampling any of the tablets for aconitine themselves. They had to resort to animal testing using mice. None of the mice showed any ill effects; they rather enjoyed the tablets, actually. Another dead end." Quilter fell silent.

"Well," said Bryce, "in view of what you have said, the information I have may now be irrelevant.

"This afternoon, Frances Anderson, one of the waitresses who was serving at tea yesterday, asked to speak to me. She had noticed an incident which, at any other time, wouldn't have been significant, and she simply forgot about it. Much later, it came back to her, and so she mentioned it to us.

"We're back to the tube of tablets, gentlemen. She saw, or at least says she saw, Farrow hand a little glass tube to Miss Fitzgerald. She then saw Miss Fitzgerald shake the tube above her own tea. Unfortunately, she didn't see whether Farrow took – or was given – anything from the tube. Nor did she see who then took possession of the tube. However, assuming it was the same tube that was secreted in her bag it would seem to belong to Miss Fitzgerald herself. If that is so, it would seem that Farrow passed the tube back after taking one or more tablets for his own tea.

"Miss Anderson had seen other people using sweeteners before, so at the time the possible significance simply didn't register in the mind of a very busy girl.

"All I'd say is this, Catchpole; in the total absence of any other apparent means of administration of the cyanide, I strongly suggest that the Dulcin connection shouldn't be ignored. Suppose that Miss Fitzgerald somehow got Farrow to take the only adulterated tablet, just as Armstrong did, you'll recall, when ensuring that his potential victim took the 'right' scone – the one with arsenic sprinkled on it."

Inspector Catchpole groaned aloud. Bryce could sympathise. There were few cases in which he himself hadn't occasionally groaned in frustration.

Sergeant Pryke finished his telephone conversation at this point, and approached the table. He silently handed a slip of paper to his boss, and left the room.

"Incidentally, we've been digging around into the backgrounds of all the group, and I think we can safely drop the two men from enquiries. Squadron Leader Fisher has nothing about him to even raise an eyebrow over – much less suspicions. He's a happily married man whose wife will shortly join him on the base; absolutely no suggestion from any quarter that he was making a play for Lydia Fitzgerald's attentions and wanted Farrow out of the way.

"Likewise for Jeremy Waller. Waller is, as you know, a solicitor, and the senior partner at his firm was approached, off the record, by one of my lads who knows him through his son. The partner gave Waller a very good reference. Said he could be somewhat bombastic at times, but was considered to be an extremely decent chap.

"The two girls have much more interesting backgrounds from our point of view – not least because although both of them told us they were students, neither of them told us what they were actually studying when they were first interviewed. Turns out Miss Jamieson is a trainee doctor, apparently fulfilling a childhood ambition to save lives. Miss Wade is studying to be a pharmacist.

"I'll confess I had a rush of hopefulness when I heard that, and following up with Miss Wade is a priority now. If she had access to the means of poisoning, as well as the technical know-how to make the means of holding the poison in place until it was administered – in a tablet or capsule, then she has to be my front-runner now in the suspect stakes. Having said which, until I've got some more information from Miss Fitzgerald I can't completely eliminate her yet."

Catchpole snapped some papers around in front of him, and continued.

"Getting back to the tube, sir. The odd thing is that none of the other four mentioned the Dulcin tablets during their first interviews. Perhaps, like your witness, sir, the use of the tablets was so usual that it didn't register. Or, if each of the four was busy talking to their neighbour, I suppose it's possible they might not even have seen an incident which probably didn't last for more than a few seconds.

"Anyway, I'll be asking Miss Fitzgerald about this in the morning, and see what she says about Farrow and the tablets. I'll also get my Sergeant to see the other three again, as well as Miss Wade, and see what they say when he jogs their memories about the tablets."

"Do you have any more thoughts for me, sir?" he continued.

"Only this," replied the DCI. "I do worry that

my thinking about these tablets could be wrong, in which case I'm pushing you into wasting your time. But I still think they may be significant. So, in addition to the questions you already have earmarked for Miss Fitzgerald, I should like to know why she had two containers of Dulcin, each of a different size. I'd also be interested in where and when she acquired these tablets – and who might have access to her room.

"You'll be asking her again whether she can think of anyone who might want to harm either her or Farrow, of course. She wasn't in a fit state to answer me when I asked.

"I need hardly say that this whole interview is going to be difficult for both you and her, Catchpole. Do you have female officers looking out for her in the hospital?"

"Yes," replied the Inspector, "there are three uniformed WPCs taking turns. I was lucky that we were able to fix that."

"Good," said Bryce. "I'm not suggesting that you are unsympathetic, Catchpole, far from it – in fact your attitude has impressed me from the start. Nor, of course, do I suggest that Miss Fitzgerald requires a chaperone. However, she might feel a bit more at ease, and be a bit more forthcoming, if a woman were present during the interview. If you hadn't got a suitable officer, I was going to offer you Veronica's services."

"Yes, I take your point, sir." Catchpole hesitated for a moment. "I think, if Mrs Bryce is willing, she might appear less intimidating than a uniformed officer – and I understand Miss Fitzgerald has seen your wife before, even though I think they haven't spoken. So I'd appreciate your asking her, sir. If she is agreeable, I can arrange for a police car to take her to the East Suffolk and Ipswich hospital. Of course, you yourself are more than welcome to be present…"

"I'll ask her, inspector, but I think I can confidently say that the answer will be 'yes'," replied Bryce. "And thanks for your offer for me to sit in, but I'm going to be consistent and decline. No need for a car, as I'll take her myself. Have you fixed a time with the hospital?"

"Not a specific appointment, sir, but I intend to arrive at 9 am. Do you know where the hospital is?"

"No, but I'll find it. I'll drop Veronica in the hospital foyer just before 9, and I'll take a newspaper or something to read in the car while I'm waiting."

"Thank you, sir. Just one thing. I'll tell Mrs Bryce this myself in the morning, but perhaps you'll tell her the same thing: if she thinks of any questions during the interview, I'll be very happy for her to put them to Miss Fitzgerald direct."

"You'll go far, Catchpole," said Bryce with a smile.

The three men stood up. The Inspector moved across the room to talk to Sergeant Jephson, and Bryce and Quilter walked back to the reception area together.

"You're right about Catchpole going far," said the doctor, as they paused by the desk. "I've seen a number of police officers over the years, and I haven't come across a single one around here who has impressed me as much as he has. It's miraculous that someone higher up has recognised his potential talents and avoided appointing someone under the usual Buggins' Turn nonsense, or someone with the right handshake, if you take my meaning."

Bryce smiled, but didn't comment. Although not a Freemason himself, he was well aware that lodge membership could help with promotion prospects in the Met, almost regardless of an individual's merits. Despite his own lack of Masonic connections, he had been told by a very senior officer at the Yard that if he didn't return to the Bar and decided to stay in the force, he would be Commissioner one day. He doubted this, but had told himself that, if the day ever came, his first objective would be to institute a system whereby every promotion at every level was made purely on merit.

Bryce and Quilter wished each other 'goodnight', and Bryce turned to the Receptionist.

"My wife and I would like to dine here tonight," he said. "Do I need to reserve a table?"

"Not tonight, sir, no," the man replied. "Just drop into the dining room any time between now and 9:15 pm. Or, if you go into the lounge, just tell the bar staff and they'll get a waitress to come and take your order."

Back in their suite, Philip found Veronica sitting with an open book on her lap, but it was turned face down, and she was gazing out to sea. He bent to give her a peck on the cheek and then dropped into an armchair set at right angles to hers, crossed his legs, and let out a sigh.

"Oh dear," said Veronica. "That doesn't sound as though you and the Inspector have solved everything yet."

"I'm afraid not," replied Philip.

He gave his wife a summary of what Quilter and Catchpole had said, without adding any comment of his own. He also told her that he had volunteered her services at the interview the next day. Veronica was surprised, but pleased. She flatly refused to believe that the Inspector had actually said she could ask her own questions, so Bryce just told her to wait until Catchpole himself confirmed the point next morning – after which she could apologise for doubting her husband's word! He went on to explain that they could dine at any time up to 9:15 pm. Veronica glanced at her watch, which showed 7:45, and suggested that they should go down to the lounge in about half an hour. The two then sat thinking, in companionable silence, for nearly ten minutes.

"I don't know what your view is, dearest," said Veronica at last. "But I really don't see any alternative to the sweetener."

"I completely agree," replied Philip. "In fact, I've advised – pressured, really – Catchpole into concentrating his enquiries in that area. I really hope we're right, otherwise poor Catchpole will, as I've told him, be wasting his and his colleagues' time.

"I believe the presence of Dulcin at two poisonings in quick succession – a different container each time – simply cannot be a coincidence. However, I remain very unhappy about how the poison was introduced. Frances said – and she is certainly credible – that Miss Fitzgerald 'shook' something into her own tea, and that was apparently after Farrow had hold of the tube.

"I mentioned the Armstrong poisoning case downstairs – are you familiar with the facts in that one?"

"Yes; well, the basics anyway. After Armstrong had killed his wife, and was targeting a fellow-solicitor, didn't he make sure that he himself didn't get the poisoned scone, and that his potential victim did? He said 'excuse fingers', or something."

"That's right," said Philip. "Now just for a moment let's assume that Miss Fitzgerald is guilty. Using the Armstrong case as a sort of template, do you think it's feasible that she could have somehow inveigled Farrow to take the only cyanide tablet, knowing that she then was quite safe to take any of the others in the tube?"

"If she is the guilty, that might well have been possible," replied Veronica. "However, look at what Frances told us. Farrow was actually seen holding the tube himself. Even without her seeing him actually shake a tablet out himself, the inference must be that he did. That scenario doesn't tie in with Miss Fitzgerald selecting a specific tablet for him."

"Agreed," said Philip. "DS Jephson is going to see the other four people, and jog their memories regarding what, if anything, they remember about this little tube. It would help if someone could say definitely that Farrow tipped out a tablet into his own tea. That would pretty much eliminate Miss Fitzgerald, even though the tube seems to be hers. Although that does assume that the cyanide was in a tablet at all."

"Yes indeed." said Veronica. "But this really is a puzzler. Now, right at the start, I heard you say in the Palm Court that suicide had to be considered, but that the setting made it seem improbable. I accept what you say, of course, because I have no experience of suicide. But would it fit after all? Suppose the tube is irrelevant, and Miss Wade's pharmacy studies are as well? Suppose Farrow himself procured a cyanide capsule or something and simply dropped it in his own tea?"

"Sorry, Vee, I can't accept that hypothesis," replied Philip, shaking his head. "Not just because suicide by poison in public is so rare, but because if he had such a capsule there would have been no reason to involve the teacup at all. He would surely have done what many others have done, and simply swallowed the thing – as Goering did at Nuremberg, for example. Putting it in the tea would just dilute the poison, and presumably make death slower and perhaps even less certain."

"Oh yes, of course," said Veronica. "My brain isn't fully functioning, obviously."

Her husband loyally denied that, and then suggested that they get smartened up and go downstairs for a drink before dinner.

"Let's make a pact," he continued. "How about agreeing that the topic of this murder is off-limits – at least until we get back to this room after dinner? After all, we've only known each other for two months, and married for only a week. There must be thousands of things we should find out about each other." Grinning widely at his wife, he said, "Failing that, we can always fall back on something more interesting than ourselves, like politics or the weather!"

CHAPTER 7

Monday, 15th August, 1949

At 7 o'clock the next morning, the Bryces were first into in the dining room for breakfast. The DCI had asked the Concierge how to find the main hospital in Ipswich, and had received directions. Veronica also listened carefully, as her husband had told her that she was appointed navigator.

At 7:45 am, they were already leaving the town, and were passing through a village when Veronica was struck by the sight of two churches, apparently sharing the same churchyard. It had been very late and therefore dark when they travelled to Felixstowe, so she hadn't seen this oddity.

"I don't know if the legend is true," said Philip in response to his wife's query, "but it's said that about six hundred years ago there were two sisters who fell out over something, and both resolved to live separate lives, to the extent that each endowed a church so they didn't even have to worship together. The parishes are Trimley St Martin and Trimley St Mary. There are other instances of paired churches," he continued, "and in fact in Norfolk, in the village of Reepham, there were once three sharing the same site. But that example – and quite possibly this one too – can be explained by the fact that a parish and a village are not necessarily the same thing. A church belongs to a parish, not to a village, and at Reepham three parishes happened to meet in that village; it was simply the ideal site for each parish to build its church. It was the Catholic Church in those days, of course, although I'm not sure whether that's relevant."

Veronica considered this information in silence, disquieted by the suggestion that family disunity might be so intense that spending what must have been considerable amounts of money would seem preferable to having to sit in the same building on Sundays. Or, if the alternative theory was correct, why neighbouring parishes couldn't have got together and agreed to build a single – and presumably much grander – edifice in which to worship the same God.

A few miles further along, on the outskirts of Ipswich, they passed a huge factory on their left. Veronica read a giant sign: 'Ransomes, Sims, and Jefferies Ltd.'

"Before you ask, I don't really know," said Bryce. "They are certainly one of the biggest makers of agricultural machinery in the country, possibly in the world; I think they also make vehicles like traction engines and trolley buses."

By coincidence, a couple of minutes later, as they started to descend a very steep hill into the town, they came up behind a trolley bus, attractive in green and metalled cream livery. On the other side of the road its twin was creeping up the hill.

"There you are," remarked Bryce. "I wouldn't mind betting that Ransomes built these trolley buses too. I remember seeing trams in Ipswich when I was quite small, but they changed over completely to trolley buses years before the war. Personally, I like the clanking sound of a tram – trolley buses are almost silent. Also, you know exactly where a tram is going – these things just swerve into the kerb almost without warning. Very tricky for cyclists and drivers of small vehicles who got used to being able to pass on a tram's near side."

"One thing I've never been able to understand," said Veronica. "When a tram comes to a Y-junction, how does the driver tell it to go to the left or to the right? With a trolley bus, at least the driver has a steering wheel."

"To be quite honest, my love, I have absolutely no idea," answered Bryce. "It's one of those everyday things that one sort of takes for granted. Very interesting point, though. Especially, come to think about it, in those cases where the tram collects its power from a sort of trough between the tracks, rather than from overhead cables. I'll make some enquiries when we get back to London!"

Veronica, recalling without difficulty the route described when the Concierge was giving directions, brought them to the hospital. Bryce was able to park quite close to the main entrance. Glancing at the clock on the dashboard he said,

"We're about ten minutes early, but let's go in anyway. I think Catchpole is the sort of man who is far more likely to be early than late."

They hadn't even reached the door when a car pulled up nearby. Inspector Catchpole got out of the passenger seat, and called out, causing them to stop and turn.

"Good morning, sir, ma'am," said Catchpole. "I wonder if you are intending to return to Felixstowe straight after the interview, sir? If so, and if you don't mind giving me a lift, I'll send my Sergeant off to carry out other tasks – but if you are going somewhere else, I'll get him to come back for me."

The Bryces looked at each other. Receiving a nod from her husband (so slight that nobody watching would have noticed it), Veronica said:

"We have no special plans, Inspector, and you'll be very welcome to come back with us. As you can see, though, you'll have a choice of squeezing in the front bench seat with us, or riding in the dickey seat behind – with almost zero chance of conversation! Or I'll ride behind, and let you two chat – I haven't actually been in the dickey yet."

Thanking her, but saying if anyone was

going to ride behind it would be him, Catchpole returned to his own car to give his Sergeant some brief instructions, and then re-joined the Bryces.

"I'm very grateful for your presence this morning, Mrs Bryce. And, as I said to your husband yesterday, I genuinely want you to ask Miss Fitzgerald any questions, or indeed to intervene at any time you think appropriate."

Unseen by Catchpole, Veronica blew a kiss of apology to her husband.

The young inspector rubbed the back of his neck and sighed like a man carrying the weight of the world single-handedly.

"Frankly, I've no experience of questioning a female who is not only a suspect, but is recovering from swallowing some poison she may have administered herself. Or alternatively, if she's innocent, has survived an attempt on her life and is in deep mourning, too."

There was a conspicuous element of plaintiveness in Catchpole's voice, amply mirrored in his forlorn expression as he turned towards Bryce.

The DCI was having none of it,

"Come off it, Catchpole. You're trying to shame me into coming along too. You know why I don't think I should."

"Yes, sorry sir. I thought I'd have one last try, though. My persuasive skills obviously need a bit of honing!"

When the laughter at Catchpole's

disingenuous attempt to alter the agreed arrangement had subsided Bryce said briskly:

"Off you go then, and good luck to you both. I gave Miss Fitzgerald my commiserations on Saturday, so no point in giving her a message from me today. I'll wait for you both in the car – I don't suppose the doctor will allow a very long interview, even if you find a lot of questions to ask."

***

Enquiring at the desk in the hospital entrance hall, the Inspector and his honorary colleague were directed to the first floor, where a woman wearing the uniform of a nursing sister stood talking to a junior nurse. The latter quickly moved away as the sister greeted the visitors,

"Inspector Catchpole?" she asked.

Catchpole confirmed his identity, and introduced Veronica as 'Mrs Bryce' without explanation of her status.

"Miss Fitzgerald is considerably better, but is still in shock," informed the sister. "However, the doctor is happy that you talk to her, in fact, he thinks it may help. But I must warn you that her physical and mental state – and her medication – may mean very sudden changes in her condition. If she appears to be unduly distressed, you must of course stop immediately and ring the bell for help. In any event, you may not have more than twenty minutes."

A deliberate consultation of the watch attached to the bib of her apron silently emphasised to Catchpole and Veronica that the sister was noting the start of the interview. Pointing towards her left she said:

"Miss Fitzgerald is in a side room a few yards down that corridor, and your WPC will either be sitting on a chair outside, or she may be inside. When you have finished, please come and find me. If I'm not here, just inform the staff nurse that you are leaving."

"Thank you, Sister," said Catchpole. "From the conversation I had with the doctor last night, I gather the plan is to keep Miss Fitzgerald in hospital for at least two more days. That being so, I should advise you that I'll be keeping a uniformed officer on duty here until I'm satisfied she is no longer in danger of another attack."

"Quite right," said the nurse. "She's a bonny girl, and it would be too awful if someone succeeded in killing her at the second attempt."

Excusing herself, she turned away to upbraid a male orderly who was apparently not performing his duties to her satisfaction.

Catchpole and Veronica moved in the direction shown. A chair had been placed in the corridor, but it was unoccupied. Low voices could be heard through the adjacent door. The Inspector tapped, and a voice called "come in."

Lydia Fitzgerald was sitting up in bed. Her face was pale and had the characteristic pinched look of those who suffer stomach troubles. But her hair had been neatly arranged and she was wearing a knitted yellow bed jacket, secured under her chin with matching yellow ribbons. A large vase of vibrant assorted dahlias stood on her bedside cupboard. These, together with the splash of warm colour from her bed jacket, went some way to brightening the austere little room.

Seated between the bed and the window was a uniformed WPC, who jumped up to attention as the visitors came in. Although police uniform was hardly flattering for any female, it was clear that the WPC could never approach the good looks of the patient she watched over. Veronica noted that both girls appeared to be about the same age, and thought how sensible of the Inspector to arrange for a similarly young female escort, who could probably chat on the same terms as her charge.

Catchpole, who had spoken briefly to Miss Fitzgerald on Saturday, introduced Mrs Bryce – again without explanation, and they both sat down. He told the WPC to take a twenty-minute break, and then to come back and wait outside the door.

Miss Fitzgerald, who had not actually said anything so far, looked from one to the other.

Catchpole had given a lot of thought – and even some worry – about how best to frame his opening remarks to Lydia Fitzgerald, but in the event he was forestalled by the patient herself. Leaning back on her pillows, in a quiet, firm voice, she begged:

"Please, please, don't say anything in the way of condolences and so on. Let's take those as given, and you just get on with asking me whatever questions you like. It hardly needs saying, either, that I want to do anything and everything that I can, to help catch the culprit."

"Well, thank you very much, Miss Fitzgerald. That's very helpful; and of course your co-operation and assistance will make our job much easier," replied Catchpole, relieved as well as favourably impressed.

"What we really need is a description of how the events unfolded, including any small or seemingly irrelevant things which may come to mind.

"To get us started, can you please tell us who arranged for the meeting on Saturday afternoon?"

"Paul and I discussed it, Inspector, over breakfast in the mess that morning. We decided to invite Jeremy and Emma to tea at the Metropole.

"I contacted Jem, and suggested he should invite Emma himself – which I can say he was very happy to do. I rang the hotel to book a table for four. I'd hardly finished doing that when Paul came back and asked if I would object if he invited Brian Fisher. Brian's wife isn't here, and he doesn't socialise much outside the mess. I know Brian, of course, and thought it was a good idea. So, assuming that he would come, I rang the Metropole again, and increased the booking to five

119

people."

Inspector Catchpole, a notebook open on his knee and a pencil in his hand, wasn't actually writing. Instead, he gave his complete attention to Lydia Fitzgerald's recount, observing her closely as she spoke. She continued:

"Then, something a little odd happened. Although Paul and I were effectively the hosts, and Emma a guest's guest, it seems that she invited Deborah to join the tea party – and Emma must have informed the Metropole, because when we arrived at the hotel the table was already laid for six. Paul didn't know, I didn't know, and we later learned that even Jem didn't know. It wasn't a problem, of course, because – apart from Brian who had never met her – we all know and love Debs. I can't see how it could be significant, but that behaviour by Emma was a bit unusual. Impolite really. Anyway, I thought you should know."

Inspector Catchpole now started to use his notebook. Veronica, who was sitting close to him, thought that the first words read 'Ask Wade'. She also saw that he had drawn a circle, surrounded by a number of smaller circles, presumably to represent the table.

While he was writing, Veronica decided to ask a question of her own. She had noticed Lydia and Paul sitting in the Metropole's Reception area as she and Philip had come down the stairs for their first afternoon tea in the Palm Court. Because of their obvious affection for one another, the couple had stood out from the other tea-takers who were also waiting in Reception to be shown to their tables. Their evident unity had struck her quite forcibly at the time, and caused her to hope that she and Philip appeared as happy together to onlookers. But, having noticed them as she descended the stairs, Veronica realised that she hadn't noticed either of them again – or their companions – until Lydia screamed. She put her question:

"Did you all arrive at the hotel together, or were some people seated at the table before others arrived?"

"Paul and I arrived first," replied Lydia. "We were shown to our table in less than five minutes and sat down next to each other. That's when we realised the table was laid for six rather than five. We were just about to ask the staff to remove the extra place setting when Debs arrived. She sat down on Paul's right, and that's when we discovered why there were six places. I never had the chance to discuss this with Paul, of course." She felt inside the sleeve of her bed jacket to retrieve a handkerchief and mopped a large teardrop from her cheek.

"With hindsight, and in fairness to Debs," she continued, "she probably didn't know that Paul and I were hosts. Come to that, Emma may not have known either – perhaps as Jem had invited her, she thought it was his gathering. But why she didn't consult him and just took it upon herself to alter the booking, I really can't say.

"Anyway, Jeremy and Emma arrived next. Jem sat down next to me, and Emma took the seat next to him. A few seconds later, Brian came in. We introduced him to Jem, Emma, and Deborah, and he took the remaining chair between Emma and Debs."

Inspector Catchpole took up the questioning.

"On Saturday afternoon you said you couldn't think of any reason why anyone might wish harm to Mr Farrow. Since then, of course, your own unfortunate incident has changed the situation. Can you think of any person who might wish to harm both of you?"

"I've thought of little else since I regained consciousness, Inspector," she replied. "The answer is still 'no'."

"What about your subordinates on the station?" asked Veronica. "There must be occasions when you've had to give someone a dressing down, or make them perform some unpopular task?"

"Well, yes, certainly," agreed the WRAF officer, "but nothing remotely at a level which would cause a sane person to take a murderous revenge. And I'm sure the same is true for poor Paul. Also, my subordinates and his are totally separate, except I suppose for the mess waiters. So," she shrugged helplessly, "unless there are two disconnected people who are so unhinged that they poison people with whom they have a perceived grudge..." she trailed off, unhappily shaking her head.

"We were privileged to take some lunch in your mess yesterday, with the M.O. and the Station Commander," remarked Catchpole. "The M.O. told us that you declined to take his advice to stay in the sick bay, and he didn't make it an order. He said he agreed you could remain in your room on the condition that someone stayed with you. That was Flying Officer Drury. So tell us, how was she selected?"

"Well, I gather that Brian Fisher called the station while I was being interviewed by the police, spoke to the Medical Officer, explained what had happened, and suggested that I would require medical supervision. Brian waited for me, and then drove me back to the station in his car. He took me straight round to the sickbay, where we saw the M.O. As you say, the M.O. wanted me to stay there overnight, but I just wanted to get back to my own room. I was in shock, of course, and I suppose I wasn't being very logical.

"Anyway, the M.O. laid down a condition. I think he sent Brian, who was still waiting with me, to see if he could find a WRAF officer. Or Brian may have decided to go himself – I don't really remember. I don't know where he found her, but he returned with Liz Drury. I should say that as I'm the senior of only three female commissioned officers on the station, it was a 50/50 chance it would be Liz.

"I don't know her well – she was only posted here a few months ago – but she is very efficient and I'm happy with her work and attitude. It was made clear that I had to have a companion, and as far as I'm concerned either of my two subordinates would have been fine."

Miss Fitzgerald leaned back wearily on her pillows.

"I realise that you are looking for who might have poisoned me that evening," she sighed, "and I suppose what I'm saying is that it couldn't possibly have anything to do with Liz Drury. She had never been in my room before, and she couldn't have known in advance that she was going to be staying this time. Anyway, I can't believe she has any reason to hold even a minor grudge against me."

"Thank you, Miss Fitzgerald, that all seems clear enough. You understand, of course, that we have to look at every possibility – we're bound to suspect everyone until he or she can be cleared from the list," said Catchpole.

"Yes, I see that," replied Lydia. "But poor Liz must be frantic about what happened on her watch. Could you please get a message to her from me, saying that I'm okay, and that she isn't to blame herself because I certainly don't blame her."

"Yes, of course. Just a few more points Miss Fitzgerald, and then we can leave you in peace. In your handbag, we found a tube containing artificial sweeteners. Please tell us about them."

"Even if sugar is available, I take a couple of sweeteners in tea and coffee. I usually use saccharin, but for a few days now I've been trying some new stuff called Dulcin. I'm told it is two hundred and fifty times sweeter than sugar.

"Oh God!" she exclaimed, suddenly grasping the significance of the question, "you think the tablets were poisoned? And of course, there were some in my room too," she cried, distressed by the realisation.

"At present, we just don't know," replied the Inspector. "But to ease your mind, I can tell you that none of the remaining tablets in the tube, and none of those in the bottle in your room, contain poison."

Catchpole looked at Veronica, and silently gestured that she should continue. Veronica thought that a great deal was being entrusted to her judgement, but was happy to take over.

"Miss Fitzgerald, we heard that Paul was holding the tube of tablets, and that he handed it to you just before you shook some into your own tea. Is that right?"

Lydia looked startled, but then her face cleared.

"I'd forgotten that, because Paul didn't ever take either sugar or sweeteners. But you're quite right. I took the tube out of my bag, but before I opened it Jem asked if he could have a look. He knew I used sweeteners, so did Emma, but neither of them used them – nor indeed took sugar. He just wanted to look at them.

"Anyway, I passed the tube to Jem. Jem looked at it, and then I think Brian expressed an interest, so the tube was passed via Emma to Brian, and it just continued around the table clockwise until it got back to me.

"So yes," Lydia continued, "Paul did pass the tube to me. I opened the end and shook a couple of tablets into my tea. I put the tube back into my handbag – mine isn't a huge bag and it was sitting on the table, so I could take the tube out for another cup of tea."

Lydia paused for a moment, seeing that the Inspector was writing again. Veronica could see that his little circles now had names in them, and an arrow marked the direction of the glass tube.

"I'm not sure what Jem and Brian thought they might see. The tube is plain glass, with no label. All you can see is a few little brown tablets. But I'd mentioned about the effect compared to sugar, and I think they were intrigued that such a small tablet could produce such a sweetening effect.

"But anyway, I want to make one thing very clear. The tube was in my sight all the time, and I can swear that nobody opened it as it was passed round. There is absolutely no way that anyone could have put anything in that tube – and Paul definitely didn't have a tablet anyway. It can't have been the sweeteners."

Both Veronica and the Inspector took a few seconds to digest this information. If correct, then Farrow wasn't killed via a cyanide tablet somehow added to the tube of sweeteners. Or at least, not if Lydia was telling the truth. And if she wasn't, then that could only mean that she killed him herself.

"Please tell us how come you have two different lots of Dulcin," continued Veronica.

"Oh, that's easy," replied the girl. "The tablets came in the bottle that I keep in my room. It's not the biggest of bottles, but it's still not very convenient to carry around with me, so I decant a few at a time into the little glass tube with the cork in the end. It slips easily into the smallest bag."

"I see," said the Inspector. "Where did you get the Dulcin from?"

"Deborah Jamieson gave them to me about a month ago," she replied. "She uses them herself in coffee, and said I might find them preferable to my usual sweeteners. But at the time I still had some saccharin left, so I finished those first. I only started on the Dulcin this week."

"Just one question about your handbag," said Veronica. Is there anything unusual about the lining?"

"What a strange question," said Lydia. "It's just rather nice silk, I suppose...oh...there's a gap in it, if that's what you mean? Or rather, the lining has come away from under the frame of the bag at one point. Coins and things disappear between the lining and the leather from time to time, and

I have to wriggle them out again. I have tried pushing the lining back under the frame myself, with a butter knife, but that was no use and it's getting worse. It's an expensive bag, so one day I'll get around to having someone lift the frame and repair it properly. Is that what you meant?"

"Yes, thank you," said Veronica, smiling. "It has explained something. I hope the Inspector won't mind my telling you, but the tube in your bag wasn't discovered at first because it had slipped behind the lining – so it appeared that you were deliberately concealing it."

"Anyway," she continued, "going back to Saturday evening, Miss Fitzgerald. We understand that Miss Drury left you twice during that time – once to go to get some food from the mess, and once to go along the corridor to make coffee.

"While she was away – either time – did anyone else come to your room?"

"Well, yes," replied Lydia. "Sorry; if I'd thought of this I'd have mentioned it before, but my brain doesn't seem to be working properly.

"While Liz was away finding food – and incidentally I didn't touch any of the sandwiches she brought back – there were two separate visitors. Soon after Liz left, there was a knock on my door and Aircraftswoman Rainbird looked in. She acts as the equivalent of batman for we three female officers. She had heard about the Metropole incident, and – not knowing that Liz was looking after me – just came to see if I wanted anything.

Very kind of her."

Lydia forestalled the next question:

"Now you are going to ask if she could have poisoned anything. I think the answer has to be 'no'. Liz hadn't made the coffee then, and the little milk jug was covered. The coffee was in a tin, of course. I don't think Rainbird went anywhere near the milk anyway.

"She only stayed a minute or two after I'd reassured her that Liz was looking after me. Then, perhaps five minutes later, Sergeant Dixon knocked at the door. She's the senior female NCO on the station. Again, she simply came to express her sympathy, and that of the rest of my team, and to see how I was and ask if I needed anything. I invited her to sit down, and we talked for several minutes. I was in tears the whole time, and I guess Dixon didn't like to leave until Liz returned.

"She was still in the room when Liz came back with the sandwiches. Although I didn't really want any more conversation with anybody, it seemed churlish not to offer Dixon a cup of coffee while Liz was getting the cups from the kitchenette – we'd agreed that she would make one for both of us after she came back from the mess. However, Dixon refused the offer, but she stayed with me until Liz returned with the two cups.

"You're going to ask if Dixon would have any reason to hate me, aren't you – and also if she could have poisoned my coffee in the few moments after Liz brought it back?

"I've had to criticise Dixon over the past few weeks. Confidentially, I find her inclined to be lazy. It may be that she'll have to lose one of her stripes – and I warned her about that only last week. But I made clear at the same time that my warning was exactly that – just a verbal warning which I wasn't even recording, and that I wouldn't be following through on it if she just pulled her socks up a bit. As far as I'm concerned, she took it all on the chin."

Lydia Fitzgerald drew her eyebrows together thoughtfully before adding:

"And in any case, when I think about it, she really is a rather kindly soul. So, although I suppose in theory she could have poisoned my coffee cup, because I was in such a state I probably wouldn't have noticed, I just don't believe she would do such a thing. In any case, it would have been right under Liz's eye, and I should have thought that would be so risky that it would be an impossibility.

"Going back to the sweeteners in your room, Miss Fitzgerald," said the Inspector, "we're assuming that you used them in the coffee. So, if you can remember, can you describe exactly how you did that?"

"Yes, I do take them in coffee. In fact, I sometimes take one more in coffee than in tea – it depends on the coffee.

"That evening, Liz had made the coffee, and put the cups on the little table. I asked her to fetch the bottle of tablets from the shelf where it lived.

She got the bottle, and I think I said, 'please put two in my coffee'. She did that, stirred the coffee, and returned the bottle to its place. So, I don't think I touched the bottle myself at all that night.

"But if the tablets weren't to blame for Paul's death, surely they probably have nothing to do with what happened to me either? Anyway, the idea that Liz wants to murder me is just ludicrous!

"Also, nobody in here will tell me anything. Can you please tell me what killed Paul and nearly killed me?"

Catchpole looked at Veronica, who lifted her eyebrows and gave him a look which the Inspector correctly interpreted as 'what does it matter if she knows?'

"Well," he said slowly, "it seems that you both had something different. Mr Farrow took in a fatal dose of cyanide. We know he must have received it, somehow, at the tea table, because the effect of cyanide is almost immediate. The doctors can't be absolutely sure what it was in your case, but it's believed to be aconitine. That has a much longer delay period – typically around one hour, but not more than two, apparently. So, you see, you couldn't have been poisoned over tea, because you weren't released by me from the Metropole for more than two hours after your tea."

Lydia Fitzgerald's eyes were again full of tears.

"How awful," she whispered. "I've never even heard of aconite or whatever it is. There must be a madman on the loose." She began to shake.

Veronica and Catchpole looked at each other and simultaneously stood up to leave. Veronica pressed the bellpush beside Lydia's bed, and put a sympathetic hand on the girl's arm, before they moved to the door.

"You've been extremely helpful, Miss Fitzgerald," said the Inspector. "We'll find out who has done this, and in the meantime please just concentrate on getting better, and try not to worry."

They had just left the room when a nurse came in response to the bell.

"I'm so sorry that we have tired Miss Fitzgerald," said Veronica, "but it was absolutely crucial to hear her evidence in order to solve this case, and I hope you'll be able to comfort her with that fact. Will you tell Sister that we have gone?"

The nurse agreed, and then pushed open the door into Lydia's room. Before the door closed again, Veronica and Catchpole heard a distinct "Tsk! Dear me!" from the nurse as she assessed her patient.

Leaving the building, they found Bryce walking up and down the car park. He shot them a keen glance, and they all returned to the car without speaking.

Deciding that the bench seat could just about accommodate all three of them, Bryce nevertheless asked Veronica if she would like to drive, thinking that if he took the centre seat at least she wouldn't have to spend the journey squashed up against Catchpole, who was effectively a stranger. However, she declined, and being very lithe, was untroubled by the seating arrangement.

"A real beauty of a car this is, sir," said Catchpole appreciatively as he settled back into the leather upholstery.

"Yes, indeed," replied Bryce, as he manoeuvred the tourer out of the hospital car park, "but I still wish she wasn't quite so thirsty."

CHAPTER 8

Minutes after they started back to Felixstowe neither Catchpole nor Veronica had spoken at all, much less mentioned the interview. Presently, Bryce queried with feigned petulance:

"Aren't either of you going to update me?"

"Sorry sir," said Catchpole. "I have to admit I found that quite tough going, even though we were assisted by Miss Fitzgerald's remarkably positive attitude. As anticipated, your wife's presence was extremely helpful to me, and very probably to the patient too. May I suggest that you start the briefing for your husband, Mrs Bryce, and in the unlikely event that you miss something I'll fill in afterwards?"

Bryce, being well aware of his wife's memory and her ability to sort her thoughts, silently applauded the Inspector's suggestion. Although surprised, he nevertheless approved – the ability to delegate to trusted subordinates is a crucial management skill.

Veronica, who had hardly got over her surprise at Catchpole's recent decision to hand her an equal speaking part during the interview, was also pleased. With scarcely a pause, she summarised the crucial points arising during the interview, and finished by asking,

"What have I missed, Inspector?"

"I really don't think you have missed a single point, ma'am; thank you for that." Leaning forward slightly so he could look past Veronica and see the DCI's head, Catchpole enquired, "Have you any questions, or thoughts, sir?"

"I have a few preliminary thoughts, yes, but they really aren't formulated properly as yet. I suppose the key point is that if Miss Fitzgerald is telling the truth, we can forget the tablets – at least as far as Farrow's death is concerned anyway. And if they weren't involved in that, then I suppose there is a strong possibility that they have nothing to do with the second incident, either. I have to say that seems scarcely believable; but may nevertheless prove to be the case. Someone is certainly being clever. And let's never forget that insane people can sometimes manage to be very devious."

Veronica interposed, "I found Miss Fitzgerald to be totally credible. I simply don't think she was acting. I believed her."

"Yes, I completely agree," said Catchpole. "And, arising out of that interview, I've more-or-less dropped Miss Fitzgerald from my list of suspects. I have a few tasks to organise when we get back, amongst which is arranging to see Miss Drury again, as well as Deborah Jamieson and

Emma Wade.

"I'll also need to get everyone at the table to corroborate Miss Fitzgerald's description of the movement of the tube of tablets. And, although I don't see it as particularly relevant, I need to find out from Miss Wade how it was that she invited Miss Jamieson without telling anyone else."

A silence fell over the trio, which Bryce broke. "What about the bar of chocolate?" he asked.

Catchpole muttered angrily to himself,

"Oh Lord; the chocolate! I completely forgot about that – and probably other points. Sorry, sir. Miss Fitzgerald mentioned that she didn't touch any of the sandwiches which Miss Drury brought her. And we talked about the coffee, of course. But she didn't mention the chocolate, and I forgot to ask. I'll raise the matter again with Miss Drury, but it may be that I'll have to go back to the hospital to check on that first hand."

"Yes, I think in the absence of any other obvious medium, the chocolate has to be suspect," said Bryce. "If you like, I can check with the Hendon lab experts whether it would be feasible for aconitine to be somehow introduced into an unopened chocolate bar. Or, if the bar were carefully unwrapped, to smear some onto the chocolate and re-wrap it."

"That would be very helpful, sir; I'd appreciate that, thank you," replied Catchpole.

Bryce concentrated on his driving for a few

seconds, and then said:

"I may have another question for Miss Fitzgerald, Catchpole, but for the moment I prefer to keep my own counsel. Let me know if you do decide to go back to the hospital, and if I think my possible question is relevant, I'll suggest that you ask it.

"Are you coming back to the Metropole now, or would you like to be dropped off somewhere else?"

"The hotel is fine, thank you sir. Hopefully at least one of my team will be there. If my Sergeant hasn't come back with the car, I can always call the local station for some transport."

In Reception, the Inspector moved towards the Finborough Suite and the Bryces started up the staircase. Part way up, Bryce turned and called back to the Inspector:

"Catchpole, I would invite you to have lunch or dinner with us today. However, you have a lot to be getting on with, and I'll initiate the enquiries we discussed. Anyway, I doubt if much will emerge today. So how about joining us here for a nice breakfast at say half past eight tomorrow? Perhaps there will be some more useful information by then."

"Very kind, sir, I'd be delighted," replied the Inspector, and with a half salute he turned back towards his incident room.

**

Back in their suite, Philip settled himself on the sofa and looked pensively out to sea. Veronica, suspecting that her husband needed some thinking time alone, said she felt like walking into the town and taking a look at what shops there might be. Her husband was doubly pleased with this suggestion. First, he would be able to keep to himself the enquiries he wanted to initiate, so that if his unlikely theory proved wrong, he could avoid embarrassment. And second, the thought of accompanying a woman shopping – he assumed for clothes and shoes – was not appealing, even though the woman was his new bride.

Taking a card from his pocket and laying it on the table in front of him, he picked up the telephone. It was a two-handed model, requiring one hand to hold the receiver to the ear, and the other to hold the main part of the instrument in front of the mouth.

When the operator answered, he asked for one of the numbers listed on his card – the Metropolitan Police Lab at Hendon. When the call was answered, Bryce asked for a scientist he had dealt with before. After a few minutes' delay, the man came on the line. When the usual friendly pleasantries had been exchanged, Bryce posed the questions he had alluded to earlier, and added some supplementaries regarding other possible methods of delivery, and about the timing of reaction to the two poisons.

"I can't answer some of those questions off the top of my head," said the scientist. "I'll make some enquiries among my colleagues, of course, but I'd be astounded if there are any data on the chocolate question. It may be that we'll have to run experiments to find the answers. Who is going to foot the bill?"

"Oh, come on Chris, you can do this *pro bono*," laughed Bryce. "But if there is a bill for any chemicals and so forth, send it to me personally at the Yard. I'm helping Suffolk CID with a murder case, but only unofficially, so I'll pay you myself.

"Anyway, when you have some information, please pass it directly to my Sergeant, Alex Haig, at the Yard."

Bryce ended the call. Opening the line again, he asked for another London number. When the call was answered, he asked to be put through to Detective Sergeant Haig. His subordinate answered immediately.

"Bryce here, Sergeant, I'm glad to find you at your desk. I trust you're being kept busy in my absence?"

"Let's put it this way, sir, I'm really looking forward to seeing you back here soon," replied the Sergeant, his mild Scottish accent sounding much broader over the telephone. "The Great Castle Street case is being prepared for prosecution, and your input will be needed as soon as you get back. But in the meantime, I hope you and Mrs Bryce are having a good holiday?"

Bryce explained how his holiday had turned into the busman's variety, and Haig felt confident enough to laugh.

The preliminaries over, the Chief Inspector gave his Sergeant a series of detailed instructions. He ended by saying:

"Be quite clear about this, Sergeant. Although I'm helping Suffolk at the request of the local DI, it's all completely unofficial. Officially, the Yard isn't responsible in any way. It follows that what I'm asking you to do is also off the record. Try to keep it quiet, and hopefully nobody will ask what you are doing. But if anyone senior to you does ask, then of course you must say you are acting on my orders. Are you happy with that?"

Haig confirmed unhesitatingly that he was, and quickly read back his unusual instructions to his boss without querying them.

Bryce closed the conversation by saying:

"I'll call you at the Yard at eight-fifteen sharp tomorrow morning. If there's anything really urgent before then, you can contact me at the Metropole Hotel, but don't include any detail if you have to leave a message – I'll call you back as soon as I get the message."

Veronica returned some forty minutes later. She sank down beside her husband on the sofa and rested her head on his chest as he put his arm around her.

"It's a nice town, Philip," she said, "but quite small. There seems to be only the one main street – Hamilton Road. There's a Woolworths, two cinemas, and all the usual butcher, baker, candlestick maker type of shops, but little else. Right at the end of the very straight Hamilton Road, it was quite a surprise to find an aptly named Bent Hill plunging towards the promenade, with almost a right-angled turn halfway down. Good fun with a toboggan in the snow, I should think. Did you ever try it as a boy?"

"No, our family visits were always in the summer; but I imagine tobogganing down Bent Hill would be a downright dangerous pastime. I'm glad you enjoyed your little expedition, but as it's getting on for six months since clothes rationing ended, I'm rather surprised you didn't find another chic gown to add to your collection.

"Anyway, Vee, I'm free of police work for the rest of the day, hopefully. Where would you like to go? This morning's trip has eaten into our monthly petrol ration – and we still have to allow for getting home, of course. We'll certainly have to fill the tank before we go back on Wednesday. But even though we'll have to limit the mileage, we're okay for a short run today. We could have lunch out somewhere."

"You choose a destination, darling," replied Veronica. "Going anywhere with you will suit me just fine. I'd know nothing about this area if you hadn't told me so many interesting facts already."

"Well, it's just after eleven thirty. How about taking a look at Flatford Mill – you know, the place where Constable painted some of his most famous scenes?"

"Ooh yes, that sounds really nice. There's a word for that scenery – is it idyllic? Tranquil? Quiescent? Bucolic?"

"All of those, I think. Although I very much doubt if life in Willy Lott's Cottage would have been quite so enchanting as might appear in the paintings.

"I don't suppose there is anywhere to eat around there, so I'll just ring down and see if the kitchen can fix us up with a lunch basket in the next half hour – how does that sound?"

Veronica agreed that it was a good idea, and her husband went back to the telephone.

"The hotel is very efficient," he said on hanging up the earpiece. They'll have something ready to for us to pick up from Reception by noon."

The couple spent the next few minutes getting ready, and just before twelve they collected the lunch basket and went out to the car.

"I think I can find my way today," said Bryce, "but the road atlas is under your seat if I get lost."

Their conversation was general as they repeated their previous journey to Ipswich, and then down the London Road towards Colchester. They left the main road after a few miles, and after passing through East Bergholt – which Bryce told Veronica they'd have a look at later – they drove down roads of decreasing width until they eventually reached

Flatford, and parked within view of some old-looking buildings.

"I'm very pleased we didn't meet another vehicle along that narrow last bit," he said. "I'm not sure what one does in that situation. I suppose the most sensible thing would be for the smaller vehicle to reverse; but for all I know, the local protocol might be that the driver with the higher social status – or bigger fists – tells the other one to back up!"

They walked over a rickety wooden bridge, Bryce carrying their picnic basket. He pointed out the principal landmarks across the mill pond – the Water Mill, once owned by Constable's father; and the cottage, occupied in John Constable's time by William Lott, which prompted Bryce to produce one of his arcane bits of information:

"It's said that Mr Lott only spent four days away from that house in his entire life – he was born in it and lived to be over eighty. Mind you, there are many men in East Anglia today whose furthest journey, apart from going to war, has been to the nearest market town."

Veronica considered the property before remarking:

"I'd say it's really a bit more than a 'cottage'. But I'm sure you're right in suggesting that life in it wouldn't have been a bed of roses in the early nineteenth century. And possibly not at any time. I don't suppose it has electricity connected even today.

"But Philip, what about *The Hay Wain*? I've seen that in the National Gallery, of course. That must have been painted here too." Turning eagerly toward her husband she said, "I should like to stand on the very spot that inspired him. Can we find where Constable stood to paint?"

"Apparently not," replied Bryce. "It's certainly set just here, and Willy Lott's Cottage is shown in the picture. But it seems Constable painted it entirely in his London studio, based on a combination of memory and sketches made perhaps ten years before."

Slightly disappointed by this information, Veronica took her husband's arm and they ambled along for a while beside the water meadows, watched curiously by a dozen or so cows. A pair of swans moved smoothly past, hardly paddling as they drifted downstream. Behind the two dazzlingly white parents swam four grey cygnets. All six ignored the humans.

The Bryces decided to turn back, pausing to look at a dilapidated lock set into the river, paralleling the mill stream.

"Looking at this sluggish little river – one of several Stours in England – you'd hardly believe it's the same waterway as the huge estuary we crossed yesterday going from Harwich to Shotley," said Bryce.

"Another little snippet for you: one of the first Acts of Parliament passed to assist inland navigation actually related to this little river, believe it or not. It authorised public right of passage as far upstream as the town of Sudbury, and created a company to manage the river and build locks and so on. That was over a hundred years before Constable's time, but presumably the work done then created the conditions which subsequently made a water mill viable here."

Veronica turned this fresh information over in her mind, and as she did so a thought struck her with some force: one of the most lauded of English artists might never have painted his pastoral masterpiece without the disruption of major civil engineering works a century before. She realised that for the last two months she had marvelled at a completely different chain of events – those which had brought Philip and her together. It was quite a realisation that the many sequential events of their lives (including tragedy for both of them), had eventually led them to be in the same place, at the same time, enabling them to become a couple.

Breaking into her little reverie, she said, "I'm getting hungry."

"And I'm getting tired of carrying this basket!" responded her husband.

Although it was dry, they decided they weren't really dressed for sitting on the grass. They returned to the old lock, and used the heavy arm of the lock gate as an improvised table, content to lean against it in the manner of those drinking at the bar of a public house. There was nobody around – indeed, they hadn't seen another human since arriving in Flatford, and they enjoyed their picnic even more for its intimacy.

"Right," said Veronica, tossing her apple core deep into a bush, and putting the chicken and ham pie wrapping paper back into the basket. "I can't wait any longer. I'm getting to know you, Philip Paul Mason Bryce, and I think that you're up to something! You've had ample opportunity, but so far you haven't said a word about the telephone call – or perhaps calls – you made earlier. Now, given our supposed partnership in this case, that isn't fair!"

She unstoppered a bottle of ginger beer and passed it to her husband, before opening another for herself.

"In fact, I strongly suspect that you have found the likely solution – am I right?"

"No pulling the wool over your eyes, Veronica Dorothea Bryce!" her husband laughed. First pausing to take a swig of his drink, he responded:

"It's true that I've thought of a possible solution, but for the moment I'm putting it no higher than possible. After your excellent report on the interview with Miss Fitzgerald, I clearly had to revise my theory about the cyanide being in a sweetener. Which was, to say the least, a setback.

"Putting aside that thorny problem for a bit, as we drove back to Felixstowe I mentally turned instead to the attempt on Miss Fitzgerald's life. You told us about two more WRAF women that we hadn't heard about before, and either could possibly have been involved – one with perhaps a more likely motive that the other. Miss Drury, of course, was still 'in the frame'.

"We already knew about the chocolate, although the information is incomplete. We can't be sure whether the wrapping was undisturbed – and even if Miss Fitzgerald is questioned about it, she may not remember. As I promised Catchpole, one of my calls this morning was to the lab, to ask them to investigate the possibility of adulterating the chocolate with aconitine. They'll report back, but even if they tell me that getting poison into, or onto, the chocolate is feasible, I have to say that I'm pretty sure that it will prove to be irrelevant.

"Going back to the three WRAF women. It's very hard to see how any one of them could have been involved in the Palm Court poisoning. So, as I think we all agree that the two incidents share the same perpetrator, my theory eliminates those three.

"I know I'm being annoyingly secretive here, but even to you I'm reluctant to stick my neck out without further facts.

"I'll tell you two things, though. After calling the Hendon lab, I spoke to Alex Haig, and asked him to do some investigating in London. Before long I expect to hear what, if anything, he has found.

"Also, after we left Catchpole in the hotel foyer, I had second thoughts. So I went to find him again while you were out window shopping. I extracted permission for me – and you too, of course – to go back to the hospital as we pass through Ipswich again later, to ask Miss Fitzgerald a couple of supplementary questions."

"Ooh, you really are infuriating," complained Veronica. "However, I can see you aren't going to enlighten me yet. I suppose you're deliberately acting like Poirot, when he keeps telling poor Hastings that he has given him all the salient facts, and that Hastings must use his brain to work things out for himself."

Bryce laughed.

"Not quite, Vee. Unlike Hercule in that situation, I don't yet have all the facts. I do hope to collect one more this afternoon though, assuming we can speak to Miss Fitzgerald.

"We'll cover the chocolate point with Miss Fitzgerald first. Then, if my rather thin hypothesis is right, you'll see what it is the moment Miss Fitzgerald answers my next question. We can discuss it on the way back to Felixstowe. In the morning, if Alex Haig has been at least partly successful in his quest, we might have something just a little more solid to tell the Inspector when he joins us for breakfast.

"I'll also repeat what I said to Catchpole this morning – that he should consider how all these six people inter-relate."

"Oh well, I'll just have to be patient, I suppose," sighed Veronica.

They finished drinking, put the empty bottles back in the basket, and made their way back to the car.

"We just have one more bit of sightseeing to do while we are in this area," said Bryce. "In the nearby village church of St Mary in East Bergholt, there is a very rare set of bells. They aren't in a tower; they're mounted in a timber cage. The cage itself, and I think four of the five bells, date back to around 1530. Because these bells are only a few feet off the ground, they can't be operated with wheels attached to the headstocks, and with ropes to turn the wheels, as in most other places. Instead, the ringers sound the bells – one of which weighs over a ton, I believe – by pulling manually on the headstock. A job that must be even tougher than the one a conventional campanologist has to master. As you'll see, the 'parked' position of each bell is actually upside down. Apparently, for various reasons the money for building the replacement church ran out, with the bell tower not started. As a result, the cage was built and the bells mounted in it as a temporary measure – but in fact the tower never did get built, and the bells have remained and been rung in the cage now for over four hundred years."

Only three minutes from Flatford – once again thanking his lucky stars that no vehicles had been coming the other way – Bryce parked the car beside a squat church. They walked the few yards to look at the ancient timber building in the churchyard. It was obvious why it was described as a 'cage'. The door was locked, and as seemed to be the norm in these parts, not a soul was in sight. However, they had almost as good a view through the wide bars as they would have had inside the structure, and both took in the extraordinary sight of the five bells, somehow wedged into the upside-down position.

After doing a circuit to view the outside of the church, they returned to the car.

"Right," said Bryce. "We can't put this off any longer. Let's go straight back to the hospital. You drive this time, and I'll be navigator if necessary".

Veronica obediently took the wheel. She was a competent driver, with more experience than most of her contemporaries, apart from those who had trained as drivers during the war. In her previous job as housekeeper at Broughton Place she had regularly driven a Morris Oxford, and had occasionally been required to drive a Bentley. Before marrying Philip, she had also driven his big Humber a few times until he sold it. As yet, though, she was not accustomed to handling the Triumph, and drove back to Ipswich at a fairly sedate pace.

For the second time that day, they pulled into the hospital car park.

"Catchpole promised he would forewarn the hospital of our arrival, so we won't be unexpected. You lead the way please, darling, as I have no idea where to go."

On arrival upstairs there was no sign of the sister. A different staff nurse looked up from her table, and said,

"Oh, you must be the detectives come to see Miss Fitzgerald. Come with me." She led them round the corner, where the chair in the corridor was again empty.

"Your policewoman will be in with the patient. Just go in. If I see Sister, I'll tell her you're here. Doctor Davies will be coming round to check on Miss Fitzgerald in about fifteen minutes, and he is very likely to throw you out if you haven't gone. More likely than Sister, even – and I hear she wasn't happy this morning with the state the patient was in when you'd finished! Please be more careful this time."

Bryce assured her that they expected to need less time than on the previous visit, and would endeavour not to upset the patient in any way; adding that he hoped the nurse understood both the necessity for, and the sensitive nature of, their enquiries. Somewhat mollified, the staff nurse returned to her station.

Bryce tapped on the door. It was opened by the same WPC that Veronica had met in the morning. The officer hadn't seen the DCI before, but had evidently been warned that he was coming, and snapped to attention.

"Good afternoon, sir, ma'am," she said. "Unless you want me for anything, I'll disappear for a while like this morning," and with a smile and a brief "I'll see you in a bit" to the patient, she left the room.

The Bryces approached the bed and the DCI re-introduced himself, thinking that in the girl's mental state on Saturday she might not have taken anything in.

"It's okay, Chief Inspector," she said. "My little guardian told me you were coming, and I remember you anyway; and of course your wife was here this morning with the Inspector. Which of them was in charge, though, wouldn't have been clear to any onlooker, I think!"

The Bryces laughed, and Veronica was very pleased to see that Lydia Fitzgerald also managed a weak little smile, and was obviously now in a much better frame of mind.

"Anyway, do sit down. As I said before: absolutely no commiserations or condolences, please. It's not that I want to forget Paul, it's just that at present those conventional remarks are more upsetting than helping."

The Bryces each drew up a chair to the bedside, and Veronica knew Lydia would have no difficulty in deciding who was in charge, because this time she wasn't even aware of what question to ask. Her husband began his enquiries.

"Thank you, Miss Fitzgerald. We only have a few more questions. The first is one which my colleagues intended to ask you this morning, but what with one thing and another it got missed.

"We understand that when you returned

from the Metropole, you refused to eat anything except a bar of chocolate. Did Miss Drury bring that back from the mess or elsewhere, or was it something you already had in your room?"

"It was mine. It had been in a drawer in my room since the day after sweet rationing ended in April. Actually, I'd bought several bars, eaten the first in one go, and then felt like a bloated little porker – so I eked out the next two bars and had just the one left. The Government seems likely to re-introduce sweet rationing soon, so now I've used up my little stock it may be some time before I have any chocolate to agonise over again."

"I'm partial to chocolate myself," smiled Bryce. "Anyway, a couple of supplementary questions: did Miss Drury have any of your chocolate?"

"Definitely not. She was happy with the sandwiches she'd brought over from the mess, and declined the chocolate when I offered it. She actually suggested that if I couldn't face anything else I should try and eat the whole bar, bit by bit, to give myself some energy."

"I see. Now, when you took the chocolate out of the drawer, did anything appear out of the ordinary – did the wrapping appear to have been disturbed, for instance?"

"Not that I can recall," replied Lydia. "But I was in such a state, and suddenly seemed to have such a craving even though I didn't feel hungry at all, that I probably just tore it open without really looking. In fact, had there been another bar, I think I'd have polished that off too!

"And before you ask, Chief Inspector, I didn't notice anything in either the taste or the appearance of the chocolate either. I should also say that nobody else knew the chocolate was there. I was alone when I bought it, and it has been hidden at the back of a drawer ever since."

"Right, that's very clear, Miss Fitzgerald, thank you," said Bryce. "And just to confirm; you only consumed the chocolate and a cup of coffee that evening – nothing else?"

"As far as I can recall, that's correct," said the girl.

"You told us this morning that Miss Drury added the two sweetening tablets to your coffee – did she put any in her own cup" asked Veronica.

"No, she didn't. I told her to take some sweeteners herself if she wanted, but she doesn't take sugar in tea or coffee – just milk. I knew that before, actually, but had forgotten."

"The milk isn't really suspect, as both you and Miss Drury had some, but just for completeness, where does it come from?"

"Rainbird brings a little jug of milk over from the NAAFI each morning," Lydia explained. "It sits on my table with a wet cloth over it. I have to admit that sometimes I don't use all of it, and at other times it has gone off by the time I want it in the evening. But in answer to your unspoken question, anybody could tamper with it during most of the day when I'm out. My door is rarely locked. But, as you say, Liz also had some milk from the same jug in her coffee."

Bryce nodded.

"I'm afraid that, as painful as it must be for you, we must return briefly to the tea table. We've heard from one of the waitresses that the tea for your table came in two pots – in other words one teapot between three people. On Saturday, how was that division done?"

Lydia paused to cast her mind back,

"One was shared by Emma, Jem, and Brian. The other between Debs, Paul, and me. It just sort of fell that way, after the teapots had been set down. I think the far one from me was between Emma and Brian, and as traditionally it's a woman who pours – and Brian was a newcomer to the group anyway – I suppose Emma poured, although to be honest I don't remember."

"So who poured the tea from your pot?" enquired Bryce.

"Debs," replied Lydia. "I remember she actually said, 'shall I be mother?' which seemed amusing at the time, given our ages and lack of children."

Veronica now saw clearly where her husband was going, and waited expectantly for his next question, which she realised could be the crucial one.

"Just think back please very carefully, Miss Fitzgerald. In the few seconds immediately after the tea was poured, did anyone in your trio say anything, or did any of you do anything?"

The girl lay back into her pillows and looked at the ceiling for a moment. Then she suddenly shot upright again.

"Oh, dear God!" she exclaimed. A look of surprise rapidly turning to shocked horror came to her attractive face. "I've just remembered, and I can't believe it!" She paused for a moment, and then broke into gulping sobs.

Veronica quickly gave her a handkerchief before turning to fetch a face flannel from the little ward's basin. Running the cold tap over the cloth, she passed it to Lydia.

"I'm so sorry," continued the much-distressed girl, wiping her face. "But you have to be right. Debs put milk into three cups and then poured the tea. She pushed the first cup across Paul to me. Then she pushed the second in front of Paul.

"After that, she turned to her right and started chatting loudly to Brian. I thought at the time she was almost flirting. She had never met him before, and actually only Paul and I would have known that he was married, but even at the time it seemed very forward of her – although she could be a bit like that sometimes.

"But the thing is, and from your question you seem to have anticipated it, that after the cups had been poured I changed my cup with Paul's. It was only because I saw that Paul's tea was weaker than mine – too much milk in the cup, perhaps –

but he liked it stronger so I swapped. I doubt if Paul saw what I did, as he was saying something to Emma at the far side of the table. And the way that Debs was engaging with Brian meant that she wouldn't have seen what I did either."

More tears flowed down Lydia's face. Veronica wondered if they should summon a nurse, worrying that the poor girl was now in much the same state that she had been in at the Metropole two days earlier. She looked meaningfully at her husband, and without speaking he reached forward and pressed the bell push. However, before anyone responded, Lydia again wiped her tears and continued,

"I don't understand everything, but I can at least see this. However the poison got into the teacup, it was obviously intended for me and not for Paul – and the second attempt on my life after he was already dead proves it. But I won't believe that Debs had anything to do with this. I really, really, won't believe it!"

She began to shake with emotion, and Veronica again moved quickly to put an arm around her.

"Miss Fitzgerald, I don't understand everything yet, either," said Bryce, gently, "but it does seem more likely than not that you were the intended target.

"I'm so sorry to have caused you even more upset," he continued, "but perhaps we are getting closer to a solution."

He and Veronica rose to go, and simultaneously the staff nurse arrived. She took one look at Lydia, and briskly shooed the Bryces towards the door.

"Goodbye, Miss Fitzgerald, and thank you," said Veronica. "My husband and Inspector Catchpole will get to the bottom of this for you."

Overflowing hazel eyes looked back at her,

"It's I who should be thanking you two," called Lydia weakly as they reached the door. "If you hadn't asked that particular question, the incident probably would never have come back to me, especially given that it's hardly a scene that I should ever want to recall, and will spend the rest of my life trying to forget."

CHAPTER 10

The Bryces walked down the stairs and back to the car in silence. On getting in, Veronica flung her arms around her husband and squeezed him tightly.

"That was just genius, my darling," she exclaimed. "But how ever did you anticipate that something like that had happened?"

"Much as I welcome your admiration, I have to disabuse you, Vee – there was no genius involved at all.

"Fact: the cyanide was found in Farrow's teacup.

"Fact: it couldn't have been in the sweeteners because he didn't use any.

"Fact: there had also been what seemed to be a definite attempt on Lydia's life.

"Question: given there was certainly someone who wanted one of them dead, could there really be anyone who would want both of them dead?

"Answer: very unlikely.

"Hypothesis: one of the incidents was a mistake.

"Another possible fact: if we eliminate the three WRAF women, it seems probable that the poison used on Lydia Fitzgerald was in the Dulcin, even though it was only a misleading coincidence in Farrow's death.

"Final fact: Miss Jamieson supplied the Dulcin tablets in the first place."

"Yes, it seems obvious now," said Veronica, releasing her husband at last. "But what you're saying is that she somehow managed to get cyanide into the cup she pushed towards Lydia."

"Yes, that is certainly my thinking," replied Philip, starting the car and moving towards the road. "Although I have no idea what form the cyanide took, I can't see how anyone other than Miss Jamieson could have put it in the cup. But it wouldn't have been at all difficult for her to palm a little pill or capsule and drop it in. If I'm right about this, it must have been the most tremendous shock to her to see Farrow, and not Lydia, collapse after drinking the tea. She was crying genuine tears for Farrow, no question about that. I dare say that if everything had gone according to plan, she'd have produced some crocodile tears for Lydia instead.

"I can tell you now that Alex Haig is making discreet enquiries at Miss Wade's hospital. Hopefully he'll find something useful and let me know in the morning; failing that, it'll be very hard to prove anything."

"Don't you need to update the Inspector

tonight?" asked Veronica.

"No, I'd rather wait until I've spoken to Alex in the morning," Bryce replied. I believe that Lydia is no longer in danger. If I'm right, Jamieson wanted to get her out of the way so she could get Farrow for herself. Now Farrow is dead, the incentive – such as it was – to kill Lydia no longer exists.

"Of course, Jamieson is probably mad to some extent, but I don't see her as a serial killer going after random victims."

As her husband concentrated on steering the Triumph, Veronica sat quietly for the rest of the journey. She needed a little time to work through – and then set aside – the details of the case which had simmered away in her thoughts for the last two days. Finally feeling the matter could be left she turned and suggested,

"What about tea in the Palm Court again, darling? And I wouldn't mind another fish and chip supper, if you could bear that again."

"I certainly could," replied Bryce, more than happy at the prospect.

They parked the car and returned their picnic basket to Reception, collecting their key at the same time. Bryce was happy that there was no sign of any policemen. After a quick trip up to their suite, they came down again, and for the third time took seats in the Palm Court. Their waitress was one of those who had been present on Saturday, and greeted them with a nervous smile. Independently, both Veronica and Philip considered asking her what she and her colleagues thought about the murder; independently they both came to the same conclusion – better to stay off the subject.

Over their meal they agreed a long walk to the far end of the promenade, and then back via Bent Hill. They felt that would be invigorating, as both felt in need of some sustained exercise. They also decided it would be a good idea to return to the hotel and freshen up after the walk, before venturing out to eat.

***

Having stuck to this plan, at six-thirty they were back in their suite relaxing when Bryce turned to his wife,

"It's still a bit early, Vee, but are you ready for fish and chips?"

"Yes, let's eat straight away. The combination of sea air and exercise has given me an appetite already,"

"Well, good as the food was on Saturday, Catchpole also recommended another chippy which is a bit further away, towards the docks," said her husband. "We'll take the car this time, I think."

Leaving the Metropole car park, and passing in front of the Cliff Hotel, Philip turned left, and they descended the unusual hill. He continued past the Pier Pavilion, following the sea front until, on reaching a large convalescent home labelled 'An Annexe of The London Hospital' he turned right and then right again. Almost immediately they saw the fish and chip shop as Catchpole had promised. Philip parked in the little road leading to the Felixstowe Beach Railway Station.

"Even though the weather is still delightfully warm, let's eat sitting in the car," suggested Philip, as they waited in the shop for some cod to be fried. "We can park at the dock again – we might even see some aircraft flying as it'll be light for a while yet."

Watching the water in the estuary, and some of the big seaplanes bobbing at their mooring buoys, but unfortunately without seeing any flying, they enjoyed their cod and chips just as much as before.

"What did you make of Frances?" asked Veronica. "Could she make it as a lawyer?"

"She's certainly intelligent," he replied. "But she'll have serious problems to overcome. Without influential contacts, finding a home in chambers is hard for anyone – same for a solicitor's office, probably. Being a girl probably makes it ten times more difficult, too. Most chambers don't have any female barristers at all. I imagine that her parents could afford a university education for her, but that still doesn't guarantee her entrée to the profession."

Veronica nodded, mulling over what her husband was saying, before turning and smiling at him,

"Has it occurred to you that in seventeen years or so, we might be worrying about a career for a child of our own?"

"It certainly has, my love," replied her husband. He started the engine and prepared to drive back to the hotel when an urgent question occurred to him:

"Surely...you aren't telling me you're expecting already, are you?" he asked, more than hopeful that the answer might be 'yes'.

Veronica smiled, "No, not just yet," she replied.

Collecting their key in Reception, Bryce was again pleased to find no message for him, and no sign of any police. "I fancy a drink" he said. "Shall we go to the bar, or shall we have a bottle of wine in the room?"

"Oh, a bottle in the room sounds more appealing," his wife replied.

Bryce asked the Receptionist on duty to get the restaurant sommelier to send up the best bottle of red Bordeaux in the hotel's cellar, plus two glasses.

"It won't have much time to breathe, but never mind," he said to Veronica, as they walked up the staircase.

CHAPTER 11

Tuesday, 15th August 1949

"Right, my dear," said Philip at eight o'clock the next morning as they finished dressing. "I'm going to call Alex Haig at eight fifteen sharp. I suggest you go down to the dining room at the same time, in case Catchpole arrives early. Choose a quiet table to the side, if possible, and I'll join you as soon as I have spoken to Alex. I can't think I'll be very long, so please order tea and kippers for me."

Lifting the telephone, Bryce gave the number and held the line, as the operator seemed to have some trouble making the connection with the Whitehall number. Eventually, Bryce was able to speak to Sergeant Haig. The largely one-sided conversation lasted only for three minutes, and the DCI ended the call by thanking his Sergeant warmly.

He walked slowly down to the dining room, assembling his thoughts as he descended. He arrived in the Palm Court to see Inspector Catchpole holding Veronica's chair for her before settling himself into his own seat and drawing a large napkin over his knees.

Greetings were exchanged, and Bryce gave a quick double nod to Veronica, who immediately relaxed slightly. She was just explaining that she hadn't yet had a chance to place any order for breakfast when a waiter materialised by their table, and the matter of food and beverages was arranged.

"Well, sir," began Catchpole, "I can only hope you have something useful from your follow-up with Miss Fitzgerald. Frankly, I've got very little since I saw you last."

"Yes, I think we may be nearly there," replied Bryce. He gave a summary of the salient facts arising from the hospital interview, Veronica adding a couple of points.

"So, from the interview, I think the chocolate can be discounted," the DCI ended.

Inspector Catchpole sat staring from one to the other.

"Good Lord," he said at last. "I have to admit that Miss Jamieson wasn't really in my line of sight. Emma Wade's pharmacy experience trumped Deborah Jamieson's life saving medical studies as potentially useful for murder. But what you suggest is that it was Jamieson who somehow dropped cyanide – but not via a Dulcin tablet – into the tea which she intended for Miss Fitzgerald. And that she was responsible – this time via the Dulcin – for poisoning Miss Fitzgerald that evening."

He paused while tea and coffee were delivered and poured. When the waiter had gone, he continued.

"But it's going to be very difficult to prove either of those actions, sir."

"It would have been. But now come to my last bit of news," said Bryce. "Yesterday, I sent my Sergeant to ask some questions in Jamieson's hospital in London. He reported to me just a few minutes ago.

"Two chemists who work in the hospital pharmacy told him that all medical students spend some time in the pharmacy as part of their training. Others may come down while working on the wards – effectively acting as messengers – with requests from doctors and that sort of thing. Two or three months ago, Miss Jamieson started to become quite a well-known face in the pharmacy, taking a very keen interest and spending an unusual amount of her free time there. Circumstantial evidence, yes, but apparently she specifically wanted to be shown how tablets are made, what binds the ingredients together, and so on.

"All useful; but what may be the most significant piece of information is this: Sergeant Haig, on my instructions, asked the senior pharmacist whether aconitine was stocked. The pharmacist said that they very rarely have occasion to use aconitine, but do keep a very small quantity. Haig asked him to check the stock

– without, if possible, touching anything – to see if any aconitine was missing. He also asked about cyanide, but unsurprisingly they don't stock that.

"Anyway, the pharmacist took Haig into a stock room, pointed out a tiny bottle on a shelf and then looked in a ledger. Apparently, the bottle was only half full, when according to the records it should be full.

"Sergeant Haig wasn't allowed to remove the bottle – understandably, as the pharmacist said he could kill half of London with it. But Haig used his initiative, and without leaving the pharmacy he called the Yard and had a fingerprint officer come to dust the bottle. I'm always saying that I'm not a betting man – while simultaneously saying that I'd bet a lot of money on something. In this case, I shouldn't bet much – but I'll certainly be disappointed if we don't find the girl's prints on the bottle."

There was another silence as waiters arrived with their food. After each had been served, the conversation restarted.

"I'd never have got here in a hundred years, sir," exclaimed Catchpole, "and I can't thank you enough. If we pin this on her, there's no way that you aren't getting the credit!"

"No, Catchpole," replied the DCI firmly. "I hold you to the promise you made on Saturday. Under no circumstances whatsoever are you to bring my name into this case. I've involved others on a 'do me a favour' basis, and I really don't want them to be professionally embarrassed – with all the consequences that might entail.

"I think you'll go far, and deserve that little bit of luck that every detective needs sometimes. Just treat our presence here as a bit of good luck. Also, this case has given you some useful experience – another invaluable commodity, which I'm sure will benefit whichever community you serve in your police career.

"Anyway, until you get a conviction in court, the case isn't over. And, as you said earlier, the Farrow murder may be harder to prove. Now, I'll give you what I expect will be my last bit of advice.

"First, get a full statement from Miss Fitzgerald. In particular, get her to expand on a comment she made to us yesterday, about how Miss Jamieson could be very forward and flirty. If she had made eyes at Farrow, that would be another bit of circumstantial evidence, especially if others had seen the same thing.

"Then, bring the lady in for questioning. If she doesn't want to attend at the station voluntarily, I suggest you arrest her on suspicion of the attempted murder of Lydia Fitzgerald. There is certainly enough to hold her on that.

"In my view, there's also enough to persuade a magistrate to issue search warrants – for Jamieson's rooms in London, and probably for her parent's house here as well. You can get Sergeant Haig to request a warrant in London, when you have the address, and I'm happy that you ask him to conduct the search that end too, to save you the bother of sending your people to London. Hopefully, a search will produce something – ideally a quantity of aconitine, or some chemicals which could be used to produce cyanide, or even a device to make pills.

"Obviously, you'll have to play it by ear when you talk to her. You have two separate offences to put to her, of course, and it might pay to switch from one to the other without warning – keep her on her toes. But I have a feeling that, when this is all put to her, the fact that she has probably accidentally killed the man she obsessed over may be enough to break her down. Good luck on that, anyway.

"Finally, if you get enough proof – or an admission – this may be an interesting legal case. I'm very rusty on the law, and you'll take advice from the County Prosecuting Solicitor before formally charging her, no doubt. But as far as I can see it can never be proved that Jamieson ever had any intention to harm Farrow. Once Jamieson had poured the tea and passed the correct cups to Farrow and Lydia, the only way for Farrow to have taken the poison at all was because of what Lydia did next. She interfered with Jamieson's arrangements and made a positive intervention. So, manslaughter may be all you can go for in Farrow's case, or perhaps only a second charge of attempted murder.

"Now, let's enjoy the rest of our breakfast,

and talk about something else."

***

In their room after breakfast, Veronica gave her husband another bear hug.

"My word, darling!" she exclaimed. "I can't say that you solved it quite as Poirot did in the missing banker case, because of course you did emerge to speak to two witnesses. But that aside, no fictional detective could have surpassed your work here. I'm just sorry that I haven't been able to help much this time."

"You really are underestimating yourself again," replied her husband. "I wish I'd taken more notice of your earliest observation about Jamieson, and how she didn't bother to do anything for poor Farrow, even though she was sitting beside him. We didn't know at that time that she was a medical student, of course. But Jamieson knew there was nothing to be done for him, so instead she played the part of comforter to Lydia Fitzgerald. A calculating and cynical woman. You were helpful to me – and you were especially helpful to Catchpole, by being present at his interview with Lydia, for a start.

"But knowing I have you helps me immeasurably in so many ways. It was only after meeting you that I actually realised that I'd been very lonely. That must have impacted on my work. Now I feel that my grey cells are in better shape than they've ever been."

***

That afternoon, taking tea in the Palm Court for the last time, Veronica saw Inspector Catchpole striding towards their table. As he arrived, he broke into a beaming smile.

"Perfect result, sir! It was exactly as you thought. Following your suggestion, we brought Jamieson in on the attempted murder charge. In interview, she neither admitted nor denied that matter, but when I changed the subject and accused her of killing Farrow, she immediately broke down and confessed to both matters.

"As you supposed, she had tried unsuccessfully to attract Farrow, and then became obsessed with eliminating poor Miss Fitzgerald in the hope of getting him after all. She admitted stealing the aconitine and making a tablet containing it to resemble Dulcin. When that didn't seem to work – because as we now know Miss Fitzgerald didn't start using the Dulcin for a couple of weeks while finishing her old tablets – Jamieson became impatient and instigated a fresh attempt. It seems she managed to obtain a small quantity of sodium cyanide from fiddling around with photographic chemicals.

"The odd business of how she came to be at the Metropole at all was indeed relevant. I learned from Miss Wade that she happened to mention the tea party to Jamieson in the morning, at which Jamieson more-or-less begged to be invited.

With only six places at the table, she must have calculated that she could arrange quite easily to sit close enough to Lydia Fitzgerald to slip her the poison. And grabbing the tea pot 'to be mother' was doubtless also part of her plan.

"Anyway, Jamieson has signed a lengthy statement – and since she made it in the presence of her solicitor, there's no going back. We'll continue with the routine work – the searches, getting statements from the hospital pharmacist, etc., but that's just for completeness, really.

"I've charged her with the attempted murder of Miss Fitzgerald, and that'll do for the moment. But my boss is taking advice on the other matter, and before she appears in front of the magistrates tomorrow she'll also be facing a charge of either murder or manslaughter.

"Now, sir, I've complied with your request to keep silent about your involvement, although that's going to make it very difficult for me when I come to write my report. However, to salve my conscience, at least in part, I've written to your Commissioner – a personal letter, not on Suffolk Constabulary paper – explaining the circumstances and expressing my appreciation for the help you two have given me. There is no mention of your employing anyone else, of course. And that letter has already been sent, sir, so you can shout at me, but it won't make any difference!"

Veronica jumped in while her husband was still drawing breath.

"I think that is an excellent compromise, Inspector," she said. "Very sensible of you."

Bryce closed his mouth again, and had the grace to laugh.

"Oh, very well, Catchpole. I can see I've been outflanked here. First you present me with a *fait accompli*, and then Vee rules in your favour anyway!"

"Thank you, sir. Anyway, I'm sorry that your holiday was interrupted by all this, but I'm certainly not sorry that you were here – if that doesn't seem too contradictory."

After handshakes, and mutual good wishes for the future, the Inspector left.

"Well, darling, please don't be cross with me," said Veronica.

"My annoyance lasted all of a split second," replied Philip. "I quickly realised that I was being unreasonable, and that you and Catchpole were right. Anyway, how about we round off our honeymoon with a final walk along the seafront, and then go back to our new home and begin our new life together?"

More Philip Bryce books are described on the next page.

BOOKS BY THIS AUTHOR

The Bedroom Window Murder

It is 1949. Sir Francis Sherwood – WW1 hero, landowner, magistrate – is shot dead while standing at an open bedroom window in his country house. A rifle is found in the grounds.

The county police seek help from Scotland Yard.

Detective Chief Inspector Bryce and Detective Sergeant Haig are assigned to the case. The first difficulty for the Yard men is that nobody with even a mild dislike of Sherwood can be found.

But before that problem can be resolved, others arise...

The Courthouse Murder

In July 1949, an unpopular and deeply unpleasant man is stabbed in the courthouse of an English city. As the murder has been committed in a room to which the general public doesn't have access, it seems probable that the culprit is someone involved with the business of the courts.

Suspects include a number of lawyers, police officers, and magistrates.

For various reasons, the local Chief Constable decides to ask Scotland Yard to investigate the murder.

Chief Inspector Philip Bryce and Sergeant Alex Haig are assigned to the case.

Theirs is a recent partnership, but the two men worked well together in another murder case a few weeks before. (See 'The Bedroom Window Murder'.)

Multiples Of Murder

Three more cases for Philip Bryce. The first two are set in 1949, and follow on from The Bedroom Window Murder, The Courthouse Murder, and The Felixstowe Murder.
The third goes back to 1946, when Bryce – not long back in the police after his army service – was a mere Detective Inspector, based in Whitechapel rather than Scotland Yard.

1. In the office kitchen of a small advertising agency in London, a man falls to the floor, dead. Initially, it is believed that he had some sort of heart attack, but it soon becomes clear that he had

received a fatal electric shock. A faulty kettle is then blamed. But evidence emerges showing that this was not an accident. Chief Inspector Bryce is assigned to the case.

2. Just before opening time, a body is found in the larger pool at the huge public baths in St Marylebone. The man has been shot, presumably the previous evening. It is DCI Bryce's task, aided by Detective Sergeant Haig and others, to discover the identity of the victim, why he was killed, and who shot him.

3. For a few months in 1946, a traditional London bus was modified in an experiment to allow passengers to 'Pay-As-You-Board'. Doors were fitted, instead of having the usual open platform. The stairs rose from inside the saloon rather than directly from the platform. On the upper deck, a man is found stabbed to death. None of the passengers can shed any light on the murder, yet the design of this bus meant that no-one could have jumped off the bus unnoticed – one of them must be the murderer. Inspector Bryce, together with colleagues from Leman Street police station, solves one of his earlier cases.

Death At Mistram Manor

In September 1949, a wake is being held at a

manor house in Oxfordshire, following the burial of the chatelaine. Over a hundred mourners are present.

Within an hour, the clergyman who conducted the funeral service is taken ill himself. The local doctor, present at the wake, provisionally diagnoses appendicitis, and calls for an ambulance. However, the priest dies soon after being admitted to hospital.

An autopsy reveals that the cause of death was strychnine poisoning.

The circumstances are such that accidental ingestion and suicide are both ruled out. The rector was murdered, and the timing means that the poison must have been taken during the wake.

The local police, faced with a lengthy list of potential suspects, ask Scotland Yard to take on the investigation, and the case is assigned to Detective Chief Inspector Bryce and two colleagues.

Although most of the mourners can easily be eliminated from the enquiry, around eight of them cannot. The experienced London officers have to sift through a number of initially-promising indications, before finally being able to identify the killer.

Machinations Of A Murderer

There are at least two reasons why Robin Whitaker wants to eliminate his wife, Dulcie. He is not allowed to drink any alcohol, nor to gamble.

Dulcie controls his life to an extent that he finds intolerable. But she is also wealthy, so merely leaving her is not an acceptable option.

In most circumstances Dr Whitaker thinks and acts like the very intelligent and highly-educated man he is. However, he has somehow convinced himself that the action of killing his wife is justified. He is also certain that his innate brainpower will give him a significant edge over any police detectives, and allow him to outwit them with ease.

What are his thoughts? How does he make his decisions? What does he do?

Will he get away with murder?